Life is a Winding Journey

Pete Duffy

Copyright

ISBN 978-0-9935923-3-1

Contents

About the Author

Pete Duffy was born on the North side of Cork City, in 1945, and has enjoyed a long and fruitful career as a musician, initially as co-founder of the famed Cork rock 'n' roll group, The Reptiles, and then as a solo artist whose talents have taken him all around the world. In 2013 he celebrated fifty years in show-business by releasing a career-spanning compilation of self-penned songs, 'The Original Pete Duffy', which has received widespread recognition both at home and abroad. He performed material from the album as part of the Mother Jones Festival, which earned him a special commendation from the Mayor of Boston, Martin J. Walsh, on behalf of the city, and was one of the clear highlights when he took to the stage at St. Finbarr's Cathedral where he sang his own composition, 'Too Young to go to War.'

He continues to gig widely, and is a fixture of the city's (and county's) music circuit.

But while the music will always be a defining characteristic, he has, in recent years, also begun to explore fresh directions with his art. In addition to being the driving force behind the Lennox Robinson Literary Festival – an annual programme of audacious events designed not only to bring the world's finest literature into the heart of Douglas but to revive interest in one of Ireland's greatest, and now sadly overlooked, playwrights – Pete is steadily etching a place for himself in Cork's literary scene.

Since the well-received 2010 CD release of his orated narratives, 'Stories from Cork', several of his short stories have been published in such magazines and newspapers as Ireland's Own, The Holly Bough and the Evening Echo. Then, in 2014, he published his first collection, the best-selling 'Old Dog for the Hard Road', a book that mixes poignancy and hilarity and which has earned critical comparison with the likes of Daniel Corkery, Frank O'Connor, Sean O'Faolain and John B. Keane. One of the stories from the collection, 'For Services Rendered' was adapted for the stage to great acclaim, with Pete is making acting debut in the lead role. The play is currently being prepared for a revival and possible tour.

Pete was one of the founders of the Douglas Rambling House. A night of old fashioned entertainment that runs once a month.

This is the third book in the trilogy of short stories and for Pete it has been a labour of love. Old Dog for the Hard Road, Pup for the Boreen and now this new volume Life is a Winding Journey.

For Pete the journey is just beginning but the road ahead is brightly lit.

Introduction

Reading Pete Duffy's stories – both in his debut collection, Old Dog for the Hard Road and Pup for the Boreen, and now, in this new volume – I can't help but be struck by the sense of unwavering authenticity, one of the qualities I hold most dear in any piece of fiction. These narratives amuse, sadden and delight, they capture the essence and timbre of particular Cork-bred voices, and they paint pictures of a time and a place every bit as rich and flavoursome as the worlds inhabited by the likes of Frank O'Connor and John B. Keane.

Shaped by personal experience and observations, they can be heart-rending in their poignancy or quirky to the point of eccentric, even zany, trends and traits that in their particular inflections are utterly unique to this writer, reflecting as they do his own slightly wild personality, his own distinctive drumbeat rhythms and his own rare, though not always readily apparent, sensitivities to the still moments in a hectic day. For a writer whose religion is nothing less than life lived at a rock 'n' roll tempo, it seems right to read these stories as confessions, because that's what they are. Even the fictions are possessed of a valuable truth.

Recently, Pete's journey as a writer has begun to take him in the direction of theatre, and that must seem an undeniable call, given the natural musical inflections of his language, his innate instinct for the dramatic and his finely-tuned ear for the homespun and guttural. Yet for me, the stories live as easily on the page as on any stage. And, if proof were at all needed, we have here his third collection of short stories, gathering tales that have already received acclaimed first airings in such esteemed publications as the Holly Bough, the Evening Echo and Ireland's Own. It's just the latest stage of a long and winding journey.

Ultimately, if Pete's work has any sort of lasting value at all – something only a very lucky few can hope for – then it is probably to be found in the naturalistic quality of his storytelling voice. Though he constantly strives to better himself by honing and developing his craft, he has no interest in trying to be something he's not. What matters, always, is the tale. The grime of hard living marks the characters he writes about. His only task is to unfurl their lives and their stories, in ways that will make us all believe.

Short Back and Sides

Young Johnny could hear his mother calling from down the road. She was standing leaning on the metal gate, red haired, a fiery woman at the best of times, especially when she was angry. Even at his young age he knew the signs, she was flaming now, standing with her faded black shawl hanging loosely around her shoulders and the permanent woodbine perched at an angle between lipstick red lips.

The day was here and it didn't make one hell of a difference how he tried to evade the situation, the mother would win out in the end. If he cried his eyes out or had a tantrum, he'd end up getting a clatter or worst still a lash from the end of her shawl that would leave a lingering sting.

At that stage of his life, just a seven year old nipper, the road was heaven, with all his friends they would play till their hearts were content, or till they felt the pangs of hunger and had to go home, which was where his mother would eventually corner him.

She had given him a stern lecture the night before, looking at him in that determined mood, telling him to be in the house and ready at a certain time.

That hair of yours is in an awful state, a terrible disgrace she uttered. She was sick and tired of dousing his head with DDT and going over his scraggy hair with the fine lice comb. You're going down to Murray's tomorrow she uttered, and that's final.

Now if there was something you should be afraid of it was Murray's the barbers. On the Richter scale of things to be afraid of, it was up there with being forced to go to school, when you didn't want to, or getting embarrassingly washed naked in the small enameled basin on a Saturday night, when you didn't feel dirty.

Murray had those antiquated hair clippers, non-electric, probably military remnants from the First World War, that didn't just cut your hair, it pulled it out, roots and all, sometimes drawing blood.

With his hand in a vice like grip, the young lad was severely dragged down the road in the direction of Barrett's Buildings. This steep incline full of red bricked houses would take them to the main artery that was the longest street in Cork-Blarney Street.

This is fecken terrible, he was thinking, scared stiff already. It reminded him of that time when they took out the big black tooth, because it had gone totally bad, a dental write off. He had put down excruciating nights of pain, results of eating too much broken toffee that was lovingly called Brust.

The mother was dragging him all the way down Blarney Street and if he tried to suddenly pull away, or act the spoiled brat by whinging, it was a side winding clatter from the back of her hand that only made him feel worst. Sure didn't he nearly piss in his short pants with the fright. With two sticks of legs knocking against each other, he felt like something you'd see in a farmers field on a scarecrow.

After what seemed like a lifetime, they eventually arrived at Murray's barber shop that was situated on the corner of Shandon St.

A strong hand on the back aggressively pushed him in the ancient front door. The mother at that stage was exasperated and in a foul mood. She'd had enough of the constant whinging.

Going in the front door, the heat hit them like the blast from a furnace. The place was crowded, wall to wall bodies, some showing red bloated faces, the long leather seats, well-worn from years of use were full with fool's like him, caught by the scruff of the neck and dragged in from everywhere and anywhere, and by the looks on their faces, they weren't one bit too happy.

There were shawlies there, with brown noses, after passing each other large pinches of snuff and the odour of toxic smoke from strong woodbines could be cut with a bread knife. Inquisitive snotty nosed babies with squinty eyes could be seen, gawking out from under the shawls.

There was a terrible smell, some fecker must have left off, and on top of that the windows were jammed solid, sealed so tight from all the years of painting,

He felt he'd lived a thousand deaths, with legs sweating from sticking to the leather seats, an under pants that was now longer than his short pants because the elasticity had gone limp many wash's ago and socks that were down around his ankles.

There were fellas rushing out the door crying from the pain and mortification. Bits of toilet paper could be seen stuck to the backs of their heads and it stained with blood

Whose next says the small bald man standing near the high chair wearing a long white doctors coat that's covered with multi coloured bits of hair. He has two silver implements in one hand and a table cloth hanging over the other.

The mother pulls young Johnny off the leather seat in a sudden jerk. He's been clung to it from the fright, and soaking wet from the profusion of sweat.

Forced up onto the giant chair and seated in the middle of the well-worn timber plank that ran from arm to arm, put there to facilitate small boys like him, hindered with the affliction of short legs.

The chequered table cloth is tied roughly around his thin young neck in a suffocating knot of strangulation, falling down around him it covers the whole of his body like some kind of ancient Egyptian shroud.

Looking at the mother in a jaded fashion the bald barber asks, "What will I do Mam?"

"Short back and sides Sir" she replies.

And with that Murray the barber commences the long ordeal of scalping.

The Crop

When crops were cut he kissed the ground.
A stubbled field lay around.
The sun had come to set him free.
Warming the land and the hawthorn tree.

The St Frances Hall Incident

We were up on the stage in St Frances Hall, a popular venue situated at the start of the Mardyke, anxiously waiting to be told when to start the first song.

The lights dimmed and we're off into the intro of Woolly Bully which was our signature tune, the curtains are pulled open, the spot lights come on and the crowd are looking up at us as we belt out the music as loud as we can.

The Reptiles. All dressed up in our leopard skin waist coats and donning long scruffy hair, thinking were the flavour of the month, Corks new kids on the block

The teenagers are already dancing around the floor like a bunch of maniacs.

At that time we could get a good fifteen minutes by repeating Woolly Bully four times, shaking and swinging driving the crowd wild, young like us they were hell bent on having a good time and living for the moment.

The girls with their miniskirts up around their arses and the lads clobbered out to the nines, a regular fashion show, everyone hopping and jiving on the dance floor.

The Reptiles had their own following back then, fans who could relate to us, because in the long run we were one of their own.

We had been guzzling bottles of Celebration in our favourite watering hole, The Double Seven, two nights before, when those two lashers in minis no bigger than handkerchiefs walked up to us and said:

"We heard a rumour about yere going to America on tour", so

playing along just to impress them I said, "That's right were heading off next week," then we forgot all about it.

It was forgotten about alright, until we saw the ad. in the Evening Echo.

Appearing Friday night at St Frances Hall. Corks own answer to the Rolling Stones.

THE REPTILES. Last performance before their coast to coast tour of America.

What had happened was that the promoter who was running the dance, thinking he'd get more bodies into the hall, put out the rumour, and put it in the Echo as well.

Some stunt to pull, this guy wanted to make as much money as possible from the night.

So here we were up on the stage acting like the next best thing since sliced pan, and smiling at the groups of girls who were crowding around the front of the stage,

Willy shouts over to me, "What are we going to do next week if any of this lot see us out on the street, we'll be disgraced." "Maybe we should go away somewhere for a week," I shouts back, then they'll all think we're really gone on tour.

We were repeating Woolly Bully for the fourth time when pandemonium broke out, a fight had erupted in the hall, the notorious Wacker right in the middle of it and him swinging a hatchet.

People were running in all directions trying to get out of the way. Next the bouncers pushed open the two doors at the end of the hall and the fight found its way out to the street.

In a flash the hall was empty, everyone was out on the street as spectators more interested in watching the fight, and we were left up on the stage, performing to ourselves.

The guards instantly came in their black squad car and broke up the fight. They immediately announced that the dance was over, stating that this disturbance was causing too much noise and wouldn't be allowed to go on any longer. We hadn't even got to the end of our first song Woolly Bully and the dance was already over. The promoter crying the poor mouth said he'd have to pay every one back their money, adding he'd make nothing on the night and would actually be out of pocket.

We nearly had a stand up fight with him, until Willy in his own persuasive way convinced the promoter it would be wiser if he paid us. We were handed over a red ten bob note, as a means of keeping the peace.

The band equipment was hurriedly squeezed into the back of the old Humber Hawk which was our band wagon at the time, in a flash we all pilled in and headed straight for the Double Seven, still wearing our leopard skin waistcoats. After two rounds of bottles of Celebration the mood wasn't that great, so we each in our separate ways slowly drifted home.

In the aftermath of the whole sorry escapade there really wasn't an awful lot said about the Reptiles not going on tour to America. Maybe in the overall scheme of things at the time it was seen for what it was. Just a cheap promotional stunt pulled by the promoter who put on the dance, to get more bodies into the hall.

The Village

The house is old, the sun is hot, the village half asleep,
I've traveled half across the world, my friends again to meet
Old people stop to shake my hand, I smile and say hello.
An ancient place, an ancient land, that I have come to know.

The Flight of the Falcon

The Great Kahn sat astride his high saddle watching Ulan the regal bird of prey swoop majestically down on the unsuspecting rabbit, hitting the little animal's body with the speed of a meteorite and breaking its back, then majestically in a graceful display of feathers, it rose again, its deep piercing talon's holding the furry prey in the final grip of death.

Kublai the chosen one, the great leader's grandson cheered enthusiastically, standing daringly on the back of his own white horse, the fire of excitement burning in his young eyes. These days the Great Kahn was in a jovial and relaxed mood, still savouring the joys of winning the great victory.

After all the decimating feuds and bitter conflicts that had plagued the vast grasslands of Mongolia over the last twenty years, the nomadic tribes had eventually agreed to bury the hatchet, fight under the one banner of the Blue Mongols with the ruthless Genghis Kahn as their supreme leader.

In the great battle that came to pass, the Mongols filled the vast grasslands of the steppes like a plague of locusts, advancing at the speed of light on their small muscular horse's, with stealth precision the wild nomadic horde had advanced, successfully surviving the scorching heat of the dreaded Gobi Desert.

With a thunderous roar of wild hysteria ringing in the air, they charged out of the black moonless night in their thousands, breaching the daunting barrier of China's Great Wall as if it were paper thin and proceeding to sack and plunder all before them, not stopping until they achieved total submission from that conquered nation in the land of plenty. The genus of the Chinese mandarin was solely in commerce. As warriors prepared to draw blood, they were a total disaster, so under the circumstances, in their humbled state they had no choice but to kowtow at the feet of their new Mongol overlords. Now in this time of pleasure, the Great Khan could partake in his favorite pastime, hunting with his beloved Falcons.

The small over protective band of body guards whose main task was to see that the Kahn and his young grandson came to no harm, had the sense to hold well back, giving their leader plenty of space to breathe. He could spend hours out on the grasslands, where he felt at one with the land, just him, Kublai and the birds, the tranquility was always a healer, a magic elixir.

The Kahn cherished these times away from the stresses of being a ruler, a ruler that of late seemed to be forever trying to solve the squabbles and infighting within his own power hungry family.

It was because of this precise reason he'd chosen Kublia to succeed him, and why the young boy was always by his side. Kublai needed to learn fast the art of war and the conniving ways of diplomacy. Genghis was forever instilling his motto in the young lad. "Don't let your left hand know what your right hand is doing." It stood well for the great Kahn over the years.

The young boy had been nine years old when he and his younger brother were out on their first hunt with Genghis their grandfather. The mighty Falcon Ulan had killed a rabbit and squawking loudly had lain it at the feet of the young Kublai. In the grandfathers eyes it was a signal, a sign from the Gods that the young boy was to be the chosen one, the future Khan.

Genghis then smeared fat from the killed animal unto Kublai's middle finger, a ritual in accordance with the age old Mongol tradition of naming a future Khan.

The younger brother ran from the scene, crying with jealousy that he wasn't the chosen one. A jealousy that would eat away at him and would in later years have the two brothers fight a duel to the death. Kublai coming out the eventually victor.

There was a new way of life on the horizon for the savage Mongols, a time to live in lasting peace, a time that would call for a new kind of Khan who would build and make more prosperous this vast land now under their command. Genghis knew it wouldn't be him, he was too much for the old ways, the way of the warrior. But even though he had a vast offspring of grandsons, he could now see a rear intelligence in young Kublai. The young lad had the makings of a great Khan, a Khan who would lead the Mongols to a better way of life. A Khan who would create peace in the spreading Mongol empire that was crossing new borders by the day.

This was the future for the Mongol nation, to hold what they had conquered, they must learn the ways of peace.

*   *   *

Later that day by the wavering shadows of the camp fire as the dusk of the evening raced in, the great Kahn and his young grandson sat shoulder to shoulder, relaxing, their backs against the skin covered Hurd. With greasy fingers they ate the roasted flesh of the captured rabbits and drank wooden cupfuls of sherbet yogurt. Resting nearby on a makeshift wooden tee perch that was sunk deep into the grassy ground, was the Khans favorite and constant companion, the mighty Falcon Ulan. The giant bird softly cooed while preening its glossy feathers, but still held a protective alertness in its yellow eyes, eyes that now reflected the dancing light of the camp fire. From time to time the large bird calmly accepted the juicy chunks of rabbit meat that young Kublai served from his naked hand.

Genghis Kahn was again telling the enthralled young lad the great history of the Mongols, while in between it all, passing on sublime instructions as he prepared the boy to be the future Kahn. In the years that came to pass, the old Kahn would be proven right in his assessment of Kublai.

He would have been proud of the way his grandson held the Mongol nation together. As supreme Kahn Kublai would spread the Mongol empire over vast stretches of the known world.

Founing the Yuan Dynasty. Kublai's realm would eventually reach from the blue Pacific to the black sea, and from Siberia all the way to ancient lands of Afghanistan. Making Kublai Khan one of the greatest leaders that ever lived.

After two hours of sitting by the warm hypnotic flames of the camp fire, listening to the soft melodic voice of his beloved grandfather, young Kublai in his relaxation became droopy eyed, eventually succumbing to the sleep that had kept threatening to overtake him.

Slowly laying his tired head across the lap the great Genghis Kahns, contented the young boy fell into a deep slumber of oblivion.

As the giant red globe of the summers harvest moon sat in the star studded sky, sending its fiery rays dancing across the great grasslands of Mongolia, Ulan the mighty Falcon cooed softly while spreading its graceful wings. Then as the night breeze softly sang the ancient song of the Steppes, the great bird of prey stood in silent vigil.

The Cripple

He sat inside the old half, door.
His body all deformed.
And in the innocence of childhood,
When ere we passed, we scorned.
Looks of joy displayed his mood,
In distance soared his soul.
A king upon his mobile throne,
The bird that's never flown.

The Ass and the Elbow

The lady of the manor was in a state of panic. After searching high and low she had now come to the realization that drastic action would have to be taken. Because of the war effort there was absolutely no horses left in the surrounding areas.

It was 1915 and the annual north Cork horse show was in danger of being cancelled owing the shortage of horses.

So Lady Fitz Morris who was the chief organizer of the event, and whose palatial grounds would be used to house the show, made the unique decision. They may not have access to horses, but however there was a plentiful supply of asses in the general area, so for that year it was decided there would be an ass show instead.

It was an awesome sight to see the men and women of the general area sitting happily on their asses.

Because of their position in society many of the high bred aristocracy had trim well-kept asses emitting a pleasing aromatic smell.

A few of the mountain men who had arrived the night before, now tired after a whole days journey, tended to have long haired scraggy asses as a means of staying warm in the cold weather.

It must be said that a lot of the farmers had beautiful fat asses, well fed and wobbling from side to side as they sashayed around the pristine manicured lawns.

The tinkers and travellers of the road tended to stay off to the side in the shade of the big house. Happy in their own company, they were already intoxicated, singing obnoxious songs and thirsting for a fight.

Now their asses were absolutely filthy, never being washed properly for long periods. There was years of foreign matter hanging down behind and swaying in the wind. The stink was noxious every time they moved.

Timmy Joe Cooney had rendered tender loving care to his ass all morning, brushing the brown hair to silk until it shone with the suns reflection, he then bent over and sprayed it with some secret concoction filling the air with the odour of lilac that could be smelt in the next town land.

Nosher Condon who was toothless had an old grey ass, and because of the hair being rubbed raw from using a wide leather belt, the pink skin was covered in a mass of blue varicose veins that depicted the map of Ireland.

Nosher had got caught in a sudden downpour coming over the mountain pass, and was now busy wiping the brown splatters off his ass with an old grandfather shirt.

The judging of asses was held in a large marquee, but the entrance door was very narrow and because some of the competitors had extra-large asses, there was a constant problem with congestion.

Murty Mcginn who had an exceptionally wide ass that sometimes scraped along the ground, got stuck solid in the doorway. He got the front part in ok, but try as hard as he could, the rest of his ass wouldn't go into the marquee.

Wacker Flynn came up with the solution, they greased Murty's ass all over with Kerry butter and it slid in without any more bother.

Lady Mezmerelda Tu Tu won first prize. Of French extraction, Lady M as she was affectionately known, had a Nobel ass. Moving slowly around in a provocative fashion, everyone could see it was truly a female ass in its prime.
Powered between the cheeks, it periodically left off blasts of scented air that floated in little clouds of smoke, bringing sniffs of satisfaction in her direction from all the other male asses.

When Lady Fitz Morris who presented the prizes, handed her the rosette, Lady M asked "What I will do with it?" Lady Fitz Morris then haughtily replied, "Stick it on your Aus."

She kissed Lady M and then in a rare bust of enthusiasm kissed her ass as well.

The crowd gathered round to see her ass at close quarters, some affectionately running their fingers through the soft hair. In the crush, Lady M got knocked over and hurt her elbow.

Which goes to show that some people in this world, don't know the difference between their ass and their elbow.

An Old Man And His Life

Sitting by his window, he's sitting alone.
Dreaming dreams of yesterday, and all the times he's known.
Memories come flooding back, and tears come to his eyes.
The story of an old man and his life.

Follow the Sun

I was talking to my buddy Mick, we were on the pier down in Cobh. "They're looking for workers for the dredging scheme over in Ringaskiddy", he's telling me, "and they're paying great bobs. You'll have to move fast if you're interested" he says.

I decided to drive over to Ringaskiddy there and then, grab the bull by the horns as the saying goes. A company called Anglo Dutch were running the shipping side of the reclamation operation.

They gave me an interview on the spot, asking questions like, "Did I work on boats before? Had I seaman experience?" I answered yes to everything, lying through my teeth. Mick had tutored me well, The nearest ide ever come to a boat was when I took the ferry to Swansea.

I must have impressed them with my plaumas because they asked me could I start tomorrow. "No problem" I replied.

Heading back out to my car, it was then in dawned on me, "How am I going to pull this off, what do I know about being a seaman?", but I needed the bobs. I was idle, so sink or swim.

I reported for work the next morning at 7. O C, in the company of another couple of fellows. After we were issued with new working gear, we boarded a small boat called the Shela at the dock side. We were then ferried a hundred metres to the large dredger which was berthed in the small bay.

Boarding the dredger I slipped and nearly went into the water. "Great start" I'm thinking, "if I don't keep my eyes open I could be killed from drowning, or worse still die from embarrassment."

What was really going on at Ringaskiddy was that they were digging a big hole under the water with the dredger, to make a deep water quay.

The dredger scooped up the mud and dropped it into the big hopper ships that were tied up alongside. When the ships were full to overflowing they headed out to an area three nautical miles beyond Roches Point and dumped their load of mud into the sea.

The hopper ships had a Dutch captain and two Irish deck hands. I was told I was to be on hopper IOIO which was the ship already tied up alongside the dredger, and low and behold who's the other deck hand only me buddy Mick.

I'm sound now I'm thinking to myself, Mick will show me the ropes, little did I know, because Mick hardly knew the rope's himself, he was like me learning as he went along.

But in any case the captain could do the whole job himself, it was all automatic. It was in any case the union who insisted that the two deck hands should be on board.

So the decision we made was we'd sort it out between us.

After taking our load on board, off came the tie ropes and we headed out to sea. It was a slow journey but it gave me a view of the river Lee and the coast line I'd never seen before.

Exactly three nautical miles off of Roches Point the ship stopped, you better come back to the stern of the ship Mick says to me. "Whys that?" says I. "You'll see" he said laughing. I done what I was told.

Next the ship separates right down the middle and the load of mud drops into the sea. I nearly freaked out, Mick was bent over laughing at me, I was learning fast.

When all the mud was gone, the ship closed back together again, turns around and heads back to Ringaskiddy for the whole process to be repeated all over again.

The Dutch captains were really burning the candles at both ends, working all the hours they could get, and when they were finished they'd head off to some late bar or night club in the city till the early hours.

The round trip took three and a half hours, so on the way back, some skippers tried to catch up on sleep by laying down on the floor of the wheel house and grabbing a cat nap any chance they could get.

On the inward trip that first day, the skipper told me to take the helm, indicating with his hand for me to keep a straight line, with that he proceeds to lay down and nods off to sleep, Mick was bursting his heart laughing and I just stood there a nervous wreck. What a crew, the captain asleep on the floor snoring, Mick reading some soccer book, and me trying to keep the ship in a straight line. The sweat was running down the back of my legs and my grip on the helm was so tight my knuckles were white. Monty Python in disguise.

After about an hour, the skipper wakes up, standing he rubs his eyes, he looks to the bow then he looks to the stern, then he starts roaring and shouting in Dutch and cursing in English like a mad man while pointing with his finger.

I had brought the ship back on the wrong side of the marker buoy, we could have run aground on the rocks just below the water line, I stood there with my mouth shut.

After a while the skipper calmed down as it dawned on him, if he made any noise about this back at base he could lose his skippers licence, with me at the helm and he asleep on the floor.
He never asked me to take the wheel again.

*   *   *

I was over two years working for Anglo Dutch. Myself and Mick became the best of mates, always watching each others backs, we had some great times together. You done very little work on board, it's that you just had to be there.
Some guys had it down to a fine art, they weren't even there, got someone to clock them in, while they spent the day in the pub, but they were always there on pay day. Hey great work if you can get it. When the ship was in motion, and if the weather was good, I spent most of my time on the sunny side of the ship, balming out in my shorts, so the gang from Cobh christened me. Follow The Sun. But hey I've never had a problem laughing at myself.

*   *   *

When the job was finished we all went our separate ways.
I sometimes met some of the old Anglo Dutch gang when playing music down in Cobh and we'd have a great crack talking about those times, and ya know what, They still call me, *"Follow The Sun."*

Calling my Name

I see her face in every window pane,
Her eyes keep shining from the stars,
and when I find, it hard to sleep at night, her voice keep's calling
from afar.
Calling my name, calling my name.
And still I dream of love that didn't last, feeling's aching to be
free, she didn't mean to say the things she said, our love was never
meant to be.
Calling my name, calling my name.

Letters to the Editor

JOHNNY ADDRESS
OLD FOLKS HOME, SOME WHERE IN WEST CORK
IN THE REPUBLIC OF IRELAND

I was always fascinated with America, ever since I was young, when my father's friend who was living over there in New York used to send the brown papered parcel.

Once a year without fail it would be delivered by the green Post and telegraph van. I can still remember the comics with the glossy covers, they were my pride and joy. The Lone Ranger, Tarzan, Roy Rogers, all of a sudden I had loads of friends wanting to borrow the comics, some were never returned and it broke my heart, that was until the next parcel arrived.

Then once, a pair of denim jeans with the ends turned up, I must have worn them night and day until they turned white from being washed and I grew out of them. So America stayed on my mind all through the growing up years. "What was it like? Was it the same as how it was depicted in the movies?" It had me constantly wondering.

I was in my late twenties, had a fair singing voice and good at knocking out a tune on the Gadget in the local pubs on the weekends. Then this opportunity came up for me.

A job performing in an Irish pub in Chicago for three months.

So feeling I owed it to himself, I grabbed the chance, took the bull by the horns and flew off into the land of my dreams, America. It was a great experience that I will never forget, I will always be glad I went.

The first night in Chicago I was taken up to the top of the Hancock Tower restaurant, way up into the sky, a supersonic lift going so fast my legs nearly came out through my shoulders I couldn't get out fast enough.

Now as you can appreciate I'm not comfortable in skyscrapers, but on St Patrick's Day I was booked to play at a party fifty stories up, I was freaking out at the thought of it. Before I started to play I was offered an Irish coffee, the recipe they said had been brought all the way over from Kate Carneys cottage in the county Kerry, I'll have to admit, after five Irish coffee's I wasn't afraid of heights anymore.

After finishing my three month stint in Chicago I decided not to go back to Ireland, I would stay and take the opportunity to see more of America even though I was now an illegal.

I found my way up to the New England area where a friend of mine had a place, and I lived, worked and played music there for the next four years. Working in the day time and playing music in the night, you'd do anything to survive out there.

I had no social security number, so this ex-cop gets one for me.

Then the next night he comes to me saying, give me that number back, because that guy is still alive.

Then he gives me a new one saying, this one will be ok because he's dead. I found out later it was a common practice to apply for a social security number while using a dead man's name, fifty bucks was all it cost me. After that I was a regular citizen, bank account, car insurance, and driver's license. I had them all, I could get anything on some dead guy's social security number.

I worked hard in the daytime, landscaping and covering roofs, as I said anything to survive. I seemed to have had an abundance of energy over in the USA. Maybe it was the lack of moisture in the air. I built up a fair amount of venues where I played the music, most of the time all they wanted was the Irish airs my grandmother used to sing. You could be doing Danny Boy five or six times a night, but you'd do it, especially when you were being tipped in Yankee green backs.

I played Chicago, Texas, Florida, New York and all over the New England area. The houses in the New England were old and made of timber, like something you'd see on a postcard, beautiful. I played in an Irish bar in Florida where it was a tradition to give the barman a dollar bill, he'd then staple it to the wall writing your name on it. When I was there all the walls were covered in dollar bills, even the toilets.

On Paddies day which was usually boiling hot, they had this huge parade on the beach were the women went topless, that crazy party could go on for a week.

I worked summer season's on Cape Cod, a seaside resort on the New England coast line and famous as the playground of the Kennedy family.

In the middle of my show in this Irish bar, a robot called Paddy O Flarthy would come out on this track built on the stage, dressed as a Leprechaun he would commence to sing a blast of old Irish song's. I tell ya this little guy had the crowd in the palm of his hand as they sat there drinking their Irish coffees, he was up there swinging his Shillelagh while all those third generation Irish American's took photos, sang along and made such a fuss over him, sure you'd think he was human. When he finished and was moving to the back of the stage, the audience would be shouting calling his name and clapping their hands so much, twas then I realized, he was the star of the show, everyone came to see him. I was just the supporting act.

Without my realizing it, the years had flew by, and it dawned on me I had been living in America for four years, I had seen a fair stretch of that vast land, met a lot of interesting people of all nationalities, I'd also seen that deep down, we are all the same, all doing what everybody else is doing.

America wasn't such a big mystery anymore, I had come and I had seen it. From day one homesickness had always been a nagging that played on the back of my mind, and without knowing it I had subconsciously made a decision on what direction I was going to take.

It all came to a head one night, I was coming back from a gig with a friend of mind. We were stopped on the side of a road in Boston and had the Evening Echo spread over the bonnet of my car. We were there for over an hour reading with so much intensity, even the death column was scanned.

Twas then the message hit me hard and fast saying to me. "Johnny me boy this homesickness isn't going away, your heart is forever back in the old sod, maybe it's time for you to go back there as well."

I sold the old gas guzzler, pulled the few dollars out of the bank, and with the well-worn Gadget hanging over me shoulder, I took the next flight home. I didn't come back from America a millionaire, but what price do ya put on the experience of fulfilling a boyhood dream.

It will always stay with me, this great adventure, all the places I've seen and the people I've met.

And now that I'm in the fading years of old age sitting in this nursing home living with my memories, I keep on reminding myself that America helped me to truly find myself, and most of all, made me proud of being Irish.

A Little Irish Home

He's seen the statue that stands in New York's bay.
He's seen the Golden Gate down San Francisco's way.
He's been to places of splendor and renown.
But his heart is back in old Ireland, in a little Irish town.
He's fought in battles, the cause he's made his own.
He's worked through cold and heat, to build a better home.
He's traveled far and wide for grass's greener grown.
But his heart is back in old Ireland in a little Irish home.

The Phantom of the North Main Street

The middle Parish was in a state of panic, a panic driven by an evil fear. This ancient area that was affectionately referred to as the Marsh, was situated within the old walls of the city of Cork on the southern end of the island of Ireland.

Mostly comprised of dark narrow lanes, plagued with the hazard of unlit gaslights and constantly in the damp shadows of the four storied tenements.

In the coldest of nights, a dense grey fog drifted in from the river Lee laying stagnant and making visibility almost impossible.

Added to the gloom of that winter of 1920 was the oppressive curfew set in place by the British occupational forces, a law vigorously enforced with the butt of a rifle and the heavy handed lash of the whip by the hated Black And Tans.

But the eerie fear that descended on the Marsh that year was entirely of a different nature, a fear from the dark side, playing on the minds of the vulnerable inhabitants who populated the local area.

Those were a simple hard working class people who mostly originated from the country side.

Speaking a type of pidgin English and still full of the old superstitious Pisog's, a practice conveniently encouraged by the domineering clergy as a means of control.

Into this God fearing environment came the spectre of the dreaded Phantom, an evil entity that was beyond the comprehension of those simple minded people.

A young nurse was rushing home through the North Main Street aided by the light of a flickering candle to ward off the blackness of curfew.

After finishing her late shift at the Mercy Hospital, she was set upon and brutally attacked by a white shrouded apparition. It suddenly jumped out of one of the black narrow lanes blocking her path, it seemed to float on the bed of swirling grey fog that carpeted the ground.

It had black gaping holes for eyes and a blood smeared gash for a mouth.

Nan Donavon the young nurse was lucky to escape with her life, with torn cloths and raw scratches all over her face and arms she ran to her house at the end of the street, screaming in wild hysteria. Taking to her bed in a state of shock she had the fear of the devil in her, saying she would never leave her house again. Between bouts of panic attacks, Nan kept repeating, it was something all in white. It must have been over seven foot tall and it grabbed her in a vice like grip around the throat, showing the black and blue marks on her neck, the young nurse added that the apparition had made a frightening sound like the Banshee.

The story spread like wild fire. It wasn't long before someone said it was the Phantom, a mythical creature the people of the area had no problem believing in. As frightening as the story was, it took on extra legs every time it was told, the people were afraid to venture outside their front doors after the hours of darkness.

A butcher boy from the Old English Market delivering meat in the dusk of evening to an address in one of the Lanes was hit over the head by a frying pan, just because he wore a long white coat and cap.

The police weren't inclined to do anything to help, they were under the impression it was all exaggerated, just the stupid Irish obsession with ghosts and things that went bump in the night.

And it was definitely of no use going to the Black And Tans. Those drunkards' bastards were only good for hitting you over the head with the rifle butt and robbing ya, while they laughed in your face.

But the attacks went on, two more nurses, one from the Mercy and the other a midwife from the North Infirmary. The same story, something in a ghostly white shroud floating above the ground and screaming like the Banshee. The rumours were getting scarier by the day, making everyone more and more afraid to go outside their front door in the darkness of night.

Then things were brought to a head when an old woman was coming back from the Coal Quay after visiting with her sick sister, she had stayed late, flaunting the rules of curfew, she was crawling down the lane by St Peters Market her brown shawl wrapped tightly around her to keep out the winters cold.

Then the old woman had the life scared out of her. After being savagely attacked, she was left laying on the cold wet ground, shivering and babbling incoherently about something in white. She was lucky to be found by one of her neighbours who came out to investigate who was making all the noise.

The local branch of the republican movement now became involved, the old woman who had been left laying for dead on the dark lane, was the grandmother of one of its members.

An immediate plan was devised. A young slim republican would dress up as a woman and walk the length of the North Main Street in the darkened hours of curfew. A dozen more of his comrades dressed in black would stand in various doorways along the North Main Street ready to come to the rescue.

They were under strict orders not to smoke. This went on for a full week with no sign of anything strange happening. Then on the following Monday night at the stroke of midnight, all hell broke loose. An apparition in a flowing white shroud sprang out of the foggy arched laneway next to the protestant church on the North Main Street.

With an unreal strength it grabbed the supposedly young woman in a strangle hold around the neck, pulling her to the ground. The ghostly figure kept keening like the ghost of the Banshee. In an instant, from doorways all along the street, ran a dozen burly figures, men who had faced death on many occasions and didn't know the meaning of fear. The white shrouded ghost was quickly wrestled to the ground and in the general melee a large white sheet was dislodged to reveal the figure of a bald man.

The people who walked the North Main Street early that Tuesday morning encountered a strange sight, a bald headed man dressed in a Black And Tan uniform tied to the green pole of the gaslight near the entrance to the Broad Lane church.

Tarred and feathered with a white sheet spread out at his feet, he had a big square of cardboard hanging round his neck, and the words on it read. "I am the Phantom and this is my confession."

When the republicans had captured the so called Phantom, they beat the liven daylights out of him till he told them who he was, pleading for mercy and screaming with a Cockney accent between blows, he confessed.

Braking down crying he told them the whole story. He was a part time concert hall performer who had been doing a six year stretch, languishing in a London prison for robbery with violence, then the British army came calling, canvassing for recruits, they offered clean slates to anyone who signed up.

They were sending a newly formed brigade over across the pond, men with little or no scruple's who would by any means possible, keep the stupid Irish in line.

He gladly signed the dotted line. Drunk as skunks down in one of their local watering holes in Warren Place, and because they had nothing better to do the Black and Tans came up with the bright idea, concocting the evil plan, something that was sure to frighten the living daylights out of the stupid superstitious Paddy's, so they created the Phantom.

The locals living in and around the Middle Parish paid a heavy price for the Tar and Feathering of one of the Tans.

In a drunken rage a savage revenge was taken, hundreds of windows were broken by indiscriminate shooting and countless heads were cracked from the butts of rifles, just for being Irish.

But the people in the Marsh could at last sleep a bit easier, content in their minds that the streets were once again safe to walk, and the white shrouded spectre called the Phantom of the North Main Street was never again to be seen.

Dotty's Pott'Y

The white enameled potty,
sits beneath the four post bed.
It fulfills the needs of Dotty,
when darkness rares its head.
Now that life has turned full circle,
and her mind begins to roam,
That white enameled potty,
brings fond memories of home.

A Song for Christmas

The motley group of peasants watched in silent horror as the soldiers burned their shanty dwellings. The only homes they'd known since birth, but now that was all dramatically changing before their eyes.

A few money hungry army generals had big ideas for this large squatted area. With the aid of foreign investment, they planned to turn it into a vast holiday and leisure complex with modern no limit casinos. Gambling houses geared to attract most of the Caribbean's high rollers, and rich Americans who would gladly invade this new tax haven of the Dominican Republic in their thousands, to spend the Yankee greenback.

Bordering poverty stricken Haiti, that was governed by a tyrant of a dictator called Papa Doc, a despot who ruled with an iron fist and the evil threat of voodoo. The Republic's only source of income was its ailing sugar cane crop. But from now on the Republic would be wide open. After the bloody army coup, the new generals were in an almighty rush to rake in the millions.

The squatters stood to one side guarding their sparse positions, staring sadly at the chaos. Soldiers in full combat gear and ominous black balaclavas were frantically rushing around pointing cocked Uzi's, as if they were in the middle of a war zone.

The peasants mutely watched, some who now owned only the ragged cloths on their backs, as the hungry blades of the green bulldozer pushed the charred remains of their straw huts, into a mountain of smoldering rubble.

Carlos Santana stood motionless, holding his petrified wife in the protection of a strong arm, tears of devastation were running channels down her haggard face. Zombie like she tried her best to give some comfort to their new born baby, wiping his vulnerable little face with a stained yellow bandana.

Of distant Irish descent she had been living as Carlos's woman for the past year. The Santana family now faced the prospect of an uncertain future, maybe a canvas covered hole at the side of some dirt road as accommodation, or if they were lucky another straw shack, but that would always be in danger of demolition from the overzealous young soldiers.

The little tropical island of the Dominican Republic was now racing at breakneck speed into the promise of a new modern tomorrow, but who would benefit the most? Only the high ranking chosen few, the lowly peasant would always stay the peasant.

The following years became a constant struggle for Carlos and his young family. Harassment to move on from the savage butt of a rifle was always just around the corner. Forced to tramp the hot dusty roads as migrants, holding down any form of labouring jobs they could find, wages a pittance, or sometimes just working for the food in their mouths. Through a rare stroke of luck, Carlos and his red headed wife Marie were eventually offered the chance to work as domestic help. They would be servants to a rich American oil man who owned a big vacation house on the island.

Carlos in his new white overalls was hired to keep the vast landscaped gardens meticulously free of weeds. Marie had to wash and scrub pots in the large kitchen, till she could see her own reflection in them. Their son Chaz was now a young lad of five who had inherited his mother's red hair.

Over a period of time when the oil man was made aware of how conscientiously hard working the Santana family were, he made them a generous offer, he would get them precious green cards and bring them back to his main home in Boston New England to work on his estate.

It was an offer that didn't need a lot of contemplation from Carlos and Marie. They quickly accepted this once in a life time opportunity. Four months later on the eve of a wet Christmas day, the Santana family, carrying all their possessions in a brown cardboard suitcase, flew off to the dream that was America the land of the free, to start a brand new life.

*   *   *

In the Irish bar where I played music for the summer season on Cape Cods New England coast, the old man was a regular.

Without fail, he would come up on stage and perform at least half a dozen songs. Everybody loved him when he took off Harry Bellefonte, playing his battered old guitar and singing in his easy listening calypso voice. That was where I first met Chaz Miguel Santana. Donning a head of close cropped silver curly hair with flecks of red in it and his wild sapatta moustache contrasting his permanently tanned complexion, Chas low sized and broad shouldered, moved with the muscular stride of an ex wrestler.

Carrying a fair bit of weight, he was at that stage about eighty and retired for the past sixteen years, living in a massive timber ranch on the Cape with Lu his third wife, who was Chinese and fifty years younger. The large sign over the ornamental entrance gates to his ranch, declared in bold broad letters......,

"Hacienda Santana"

Chas had made his fortune working in landscape construction. He had originally inherited the small family business from his father and with a keen eye expanded it to the stage where he was earning big bucks designing prize winning golf courses.

A song that I was always requested to sing by the Irish Americans who frequented the holiday bar, was a song I wrote myself called Broad Lane. It was about my grandparents having to move from the centre of Cork City up to the high elevation of the north side when they were very old. All because their house had been demolished to make way for a new church, they were forced to pull up roots.

When I sang this song, the tears would be running down Chaz's face as he tried to sing along.

I remember once asking Chaz why he got so emotional when I sang Broad Lane. That was when he told me about his family history.

*　*　*

After getting over the culture shock of moving from the Dominican Republic to America, the Santana family grew into the routine of working for the oil man in his Boston mansion. This gave them the true sense of security that they always craved for in life, helping them to thrive so much that after another five years Carlos became confident enough to take the plunge and become independent. He started his own small landscape company and they moved into their own apartment. Their growing son was attending the local multi ethnic school at that stage. Because he was a natural at sport, loving the brawling side of American football, Chaz was easily accepted by his fellow students and he happily integrated into the American way of life. Chaz told me he had the warm influence of an Irish mother and a strong Latino father when he was growing up and he loved both cultures, been constantly told to be proud of who he was. His mother spoke many times about how they were savagely evicted from their straw hut back on the island of the Dominican Republic and he a mere baby in her arms, as she watched her home go up in flames, an image that always made her feel insecure and was a trauma that stayed with her all of her life. This Chaz told me was why he got so emotional when he heard me singing Broad Lane. He could relate to the song, it brought memories of his mother's story flooding back. Up till the day she died, in her heart she was still a simple country girl from the island. One night Chaz asked me would I write out the words of Broad Lane which I was only too glad to do because I knew how much the song meant to him.

In this Irish pub where I played on Cape Cod on the last night of every summer month we would have crazy parties, where everyone would dress up in fancy dress depending on the theme of the night.

Because the Americans have a zany way of looking at life at the best of times, on the final night of the holiday season we would hold a Christmas going home party in the heat of the summer. Fake snow, crazy games and presents galore where everyone who attended would dress up as Santa Claus, we even had Santa's in sexy miniskirts. The place would be jointed people having one hell of a Christmas ball, going around unashamedly letting their hair down and feeling no pain.

In the middle of one of those wild night's the chant went up for Chaz Santana to do his Harry Bellefonte act, the crowd just loved to hear him sing. Up jumps Chaz with his battered old guitar, dressed as Santa but wearing a red sombrero and a holster and two guns, just like some Mexican bandito. He proceeds to give such a magic rendition of songs like Island In the Sun and Mary Ann, that he had the whole of the audience roaring their heads off for more.

At the end of the set he announces he had a very special song to sing and asked for complete silence, then he started singing Broad Lane with a Latin tempo and such a sweet voice it blew everybody away. There wasn't a dry eye in the bar including mine. He had taken my song and made it his own and when he finished he had to sing it once more for the large crowd in the bar. Even though a lot of years have passed since that memorable night on Cape Cod, in my mind's eye I can still hear the emotional words Chaz said to the crowd before he left the stage.

With tears in his eyes he told us, that was for Mama and Papa Santana.

Heading Back to Sea

The fishing boats are by the quay,
the wind is blowing strong.
It's time for men to take a rest,
time for drink and song.
Nets are stored, fish are sold,
and life is good and free.
When Mondays dawn comes round again,
where heading back to sea.

No Rest for the Wicked

Sally cleared the remains on the plates from the table, the six burly truckers had eaten like pigs, scraps of food littered the floor like the aftermath of some animal kill, but that was part and parcel of the job, and the bonus in any case was the big tip they left.
Sally wiped the sheen of perspiration from her brow. Another day in the roadside diner and like all the other days on the Vegas strip, as hot as hell. You earned your bucks here thought Sally, no rest for the wicked, fifty years old now her pins were acting up like hell again. They troubled her a lot since she started working those long shifts. These days her body kept reminding her she wasn't that pretty little young thing that left the farm back in Nebraska anymore.

When it came round, Sally grabbed her fifteen minute break with both hands, flopping her weary bones down on an old timber crate in the back yard, she broke open her second pack of strong Camel, inhaling long and greedily, the instant blast of nicotine bit like a hot furnace into the back of her throat, giving her an instant high and bringing on the raking cough that had taken up permanent residence in her chest.
Thirty years today, that's when she'd left her friends and family in that little hick town in Nebraska, full of the notions of making it big, all because she had won some local beauty contest. She was full of herself back then, had all the young boys chasing after her, thinking she was the next Marilyn and her friends convincing her she had the looks to make it happen big time. She believed only

what she wanted to hear. Her father was the wise one back then, a dirt poor farmer, telling her, Sally girl you take care, use your head and keep those feet on the ground.

But would she listen to him, not in a life time, young Sally Grey was full of her own fancy ideas. When she got off the greyhound bus and saw Las Vegas for the first time, it blew her mind. Everything was so big and flashy and people seemed to be moving around so fast, it put her head in a spin, forcing her to sit on a bench at the side of the road. "Ah life" thought Sally. With the half a dozen promotional black and white photos and the dollars in her pocket from her savings, Sally thought she could conquer the world, there and then, little did she know.

Three broken marriages and two abortions all because she was a sucker for getting involved with the wrong kind of man, she trusted everyone at the start especially those who claimed they could help her advance her nonexistent career, she learned fast that in this town everyone was on the con. Sally realized fast that Vegas was bursting at its seems with star struck young things like herself wanting to be made into stars, and the only tools they had to achieve it were a pretty face and a young vulnerable body.

Looking back now at how she walked the leather soles off her shoes, chasing promises, getting some small jobs doing ads for things like coffee or soap where the money was crap and the jobs few and far between. In the end what little savings she had were dwindling down to nothing, so to survive she done what rest of the star struck girls done, and reverted to stripping for tips and meals. After that it was a downward trip for Sally moving from one flea pit joint to another, still dreaming she might make it big, as the worry lines took over her face and her body quickly lost its youth. Many times Sally thought of going back home, initially she felt she would eventually make it big and she could make a trip home in all her glory, then as time went by she started to lie in the letters she wrote home, saying life was going great for her in Vegas.

As time went by she felt she would never go home. When her body lost its youth and started sagging, Sally starting turning tricks to make ends meet as life turned her into a hardened woman, who depended on the uppers and downers mixed into the booze to get through the day.

After being arrested for prostitution with possession Sally spent many times behind bars, it was one of those times it hit her how low she had falling, and if she didn't pull herself together she'd end up in the city morgue. On being released she was offered a place in a rehabilitation programme which she accepted. She was now six weeks clean and her mind in a clearer state then she had being in a long time, working in the diner was part of the rehab programme and she felt proud of how she was coping.

Sally was now having a strong yearning to go back to the old home stead and see how things were, her parents were very old now, she hadn't seen them in a life time, her only communication over the years being through the letters she sent and received.

Sally felt in her heart the home coming would be a great occasion for everyone.

The chef was shouting from the kitchen, something about customers needing to be served, it brought Sally out of her day dreaming. She stood up and stretched, feeling the weariness in her bones. taking a last long drag on the Camel cigarette.

She stubbed it out under her shoe, giving out a long sigh, whispering to herself while chuckling a large smile, "Ah sure I suppose in this life, there's no rest for the wicked".
All of a sudden, a racking cough took hold of her, almost sending her ribs out through her chest, she doubled over in a dizzy spell fighting hard to draw breath.
With a sense of panic, she sat back down on the old crate wiping the spittle from her mouth with the back of her hand. And for the second time that week Sally looked in horror at the long red smear of blood mixed in the spittle. Burying her head deep in her hands Sally cried.

No Worries

A bag of chips was my delight,
as I left the Sem's on a Sunday night,
and made my way up the Northern rise,
to the place that I called home
Durango kid had done his deed,
Bad men caught, good men freed,
and greasy newspaper thrown on the street,
as I walked in my front door.

The Great Divide

Monty lounged on the jaded rocking chair, swaying to and fro on the sun bleached deck of his log cabin, gazing out over the flat land. In this part of Texas you could see to the far off horizon. Pushing the sweat stained Stetson to the back of his bald head, the old timer took a long hard drag on his Cuban cigar, leaving the tobacco smoke slowly escape through the gaps in his clenched teeth in an act of sheer pleasure.

The apparition he'd been observing for the last hour slowly moving up the long dusty road was now coming into focus and approaching his cabin.

Some crazy looking dude thought Monty, wearing a long white coat, no shoes, a turban and a long timber pole over his shoulder that looked like hickory with a cloth bag hanging from its end.

Standing and stretching to his full six feet, the old timer gazed down at the crazy man now standing before him. "Where the hell in all that's holy did you come from?" uttered Monty.

In broken English, the crazy man replied, and as if praying, he joined his hands together and bowed, stating, "I come from the land of India many many moons away from here kind Sir."

"And what are ya doing walking around out here in the middle of Texas with no shoes on?" asked Monty. "I see sign for your cabin far back on road and I come to ask kind Sir, please if I could have some water to drink." Monty slapped his Stetson on his knee raising a cloud of dust, "Well tickle me pink" he said laughing, "You walked the whole five miles from the main road in this heat just for a drink of water."

The old timer invited the Indian man into the coolness of the cabin and sat him down at the table, he then gave him a large picture of water to quench his thirst, and taking a melon from the cold box, Monty cut it into slices and laid it on the table between the two of them, indicating to the traveler to get dug in. Monty was glad of the company. Since his wife passed away ten years ago he was on his own out here, not many people came up this way. Sometimes it got lonely. Monty had worked as a cow hand over at the big double T ranch most all of his adult life. He was the top foreman there when he had to retire prematurely to nurse his sick wife. That's when he bought the patch of land and built the log cabin. Since he was a kid back in the old country, he always wanted to be a cowboy, so when he hit the age of twenty he emigrated to the U S of A, made his way down to Texas where all his cowboy heroes came from and never looked back. The Indian man turned out to be great company for Monty, the traveler said his name was Madi and that he was a holy man devoting his life to gaining the knowledge of enlightenment. Madi had been ordered by his guru to walk around the world bare foot, and that when he felt he could see through the third eye of knowledge he was to return to India and become a guru. Monty was deeply engrossed by all the conversations he had with the Indian. They would spend long hours learning about each other, and he told Madi he could stay in the cabin for as long as he wished.

Over the following days Monty became fascinated by what the traveler said.

The holy man could survive for days without food, all he needed was water to sustain himself. He would spend hours every day in meditation, sitting in the shade of the deck. Madi held there in the posture of lotus position or laying flat on his back, prayed without moving.

Full of questions now, the old timer asked the holy man what was happening when he was in those positions. Answering the holy man said, in the lotus position I merge with the great white light which is pure energy, it cleans my body and mind and gives me sustenance to go on. "And what about when you're laying down?" asked Monty. That is a very special power answered the holy man. "When I am laying down I am in a state of astral travel." "What's that?" asked Monty. "I can leave my body" said Madi, "I can go back to my home land and see if everything is ok with my people, I can go to the past or the future and distance is not a problem." The old timer made no more comments, thinking to himself, "Was this so called holy man a nutter?" so he turned his attention to doing some chores around the cabin.

Eventually the holy man told Monty he would be leaving, saying he must proceed with his journey around the world. He then told the old timer if there was any favour he could do for him, all he had to do was ask, he wanted to pay back for the hospitality that was showed to him. At the table that night Monty asked the holy man to show him how to meditate. The old timer had never experience such relaxation in all his life, after the holy man told him the secret mantra he should recite silently to himself.

Monty sat in his rocking chair, closed his eyes and after a short period found himself in a state of such complete calm, he wasn't even aware of his own body. Coming out of the trance after half an hour, the old timer was so refreshed he could hardly believe it, the holy man told Monty the calm he had been in was called the state of transcendental meditation. It was an ancient way of praying and rejuvenating the body.

That night sitting at the table, the holy man said to Monty, "If you so wish my friend, before I leave you, I will show you how to levitate from your body and astral travel." Restless in his bunk, the old timer spent many hours awake that night thinking over and over. Did he want to do this? The dawn found Monty laying flat on his back listening to the soft words of the holy man. "Close your eyes my friend, breathe in and out slowly and keep silently repeating your mantra." The holy man had his hands resting on Monty's head as a means of transferring energy to the old timer. He was also reciting his own powerful mantra. Monty the old timer awoke from the white light.

Opening his eyes, he found himself standing with his back to the wall of the general post office in Cork City. The cars that were passing on the street were mostly painted black, all the men walking by were wearing suits, the girls were dressed in very short skirts, Monty quickly realized he was back in the 60s when he was a teenager, but standing there watching in amazement, he himself was still an old man, and still dressed in his cowboy denim gear. It had always been his dream, a longing to be able to go back once again and visit his old mates, the gang he was reared with since he was a kid, all the way up to the time when they used to go drinking in the Long Valley Bar.

All of a sudden Monty knew why he was here. After a period of observing what was going on around him, and he getting curious looks especially his Texas Stetson, Monty walked down Winthrop

Street and in the double doors of the Long Valley Bar.

After coming in from the sunshine, the interior seemed dark. The heels of the old timers cowboy boots scraped hard on the timber floor as he walked all of his six foot frame up to the bar counter. Pulling a ten dollar bill from his pocket Monty slapped it on the counter as he sat on the high stool. A Bud please he indicated to the barman standing in the long white coat.

The old timer could observe all of the bar by looking in the long mirror that ran the length of the wall behind the counter. He could see every eye in the bar was curiously focused on him, especially the group of teenagers sitting at the round table in the corner. He recognized the faces straight off, his old buddies.

Looking at them now through the mirror he could see they hadn't changed a bit and they hadn't a clue who he was. Monty was happy just to sit there for the time being and soak up the old atmosphere. The memories were flooding back to him now. He had been reared up with that gang since he was a knee high nipper, until he left for America when he was 20, to them he would have been known as Shammie, it was when he started working on the ranch out in Texas that he got for some unknown reason christened Monty, and it stuck. A young teenager came in the main door and walked up to the lads at the table, donning long hair dressed in a Beatle suit and trying hard to balance on the Cuban heels of his boots.

A hushed conversation took hold of the group and Monty could see through the mirror's reflection the new comer turning and looking in his direction.

The old-timer nearly fell off the high stool, he gripped the bar counter to steady himself as he looked on in disbelief.

Monty was looking at himself when he was a teenager. Monty was on his second Bud, drinking straight by the neck when his younger self came over and stood beside him.

"Hello Sir" said the teenager, "My name is Shammie and I was admiring your cowboy hat." "Pleased to meet you" answered Monty and they both shook hands. "Are you from America" asked Shammie?

"Sure am" said Monty, "I'm from the mighty state of Texas."

"Have ye cowboys there?" asked Shammie? "Every ones a cowboy in Texas Son, we have the biggest ranches in all of America, beef as far as the eye can see." "God I'd love that" said Shammie, "Ever since I can remember, I wanted to be a cowboy. It's my dream. Some day I'm going to go to America and make that dream happen" said the young lad.

In that sudden moment they were both looking at each other with a look of recognition, and even thought they were looking at each other, there was something far away in their eyes as they both saw their destiny.

In a flash, the shining white light took hold of Monty, and when it cleared away like the melting of a fog, he was laying on the parched deck of his old log cabin and steering up at the angelic face of the Indian holy man.

She Gave Me A Smile

They sat her on a chair outside the door.
Sheltered in the shade from burning sun.
And, I used to see her once a year.
In the weeks that I would spend out in Taiwan.
Though she never spoke a word or made a sound.
As Id passed her by, a smile came to her face.
One day I heard that she was there no more,
And that smile of hers had left without a trace.

Hong Kong Billy Boys

William was laying on the narrow cot pressing his hands over his ears in an effort to keep out the hurtful sounds of his mother's screams. She was being punched again by her husband, it was a regular scene. Every time he'd fall in the door, a chronic alcoholic out of his mind from too much cider, he'd rape the poor woman and after that beat the living daylights out of her.

William tried to defend his mother many times, ending up getting the buckle end of the leather belt across his young back.

A year since his father had lost his job in the butter market, then the man had turned from a quite church goer into a raging maniac, the demon's that had lain dormant in his genes now constantly coming out to brutalize his family, in their little house in Cork's Coal Quay.

But tonight was one to many beatings for the mother, she screamed like never before, laying in a fetal ball on the cold flag stoned floor, pulling her shawl over her head as a means of protection, but with her scarred legs exposed, and the husband lashing her with the leather belt with all his might.

Twisting and turning in his narrow cot in an effort to keep out the sounds, an explosive rage of red mist suddenly took hold of the young boy. It had being building up to this over a period of time, in a mad urge now rushing into the kitchen he grabbed the hot iron poker from the hearth of the fire place and repeatedly hit his father over the head.

The metal bar cracked the fathers skull opening up a deep cavity. The man collapsed to the floor where blood instantly gushed from his nose and mouth forming a sticky pool around him.

William helped his mother up and sat her on a chair, her face was a mass of bruises, and her eyes were black and blue with one of them almost closed.

When the mother saw what the boy had done her hand went to her mouth. She knew what would happen if the constabulary got hold of him and they wouldn't care that he was only fourteen years old. The law would still hang him, no use in saying that he was defending his mother against an alcoholic brute, because if the truth be known, it was a man's world. Quickly coming to her senses the mother put together some cloths and food, pushing what money she possessed in the young lads pocket she explained to him that he had to run, run fast and far.

The mother held her young son in a protective embrace, kissing him on both eyes and affectionately running her hands through his head of red hair, telling him "Son I'll take the blame for this, you have your whole life ahead of you", kissing him again with tears in her eyes she said, "My darling Son it doesn't matter where you end up don't ever come back to Cork, but always remember I will never stop loving you till the day I die."

William headed for the one place he was familiar with, the docks. He used to spent many hours down there looking at the sail ships, day dreaming and wandering where they came from and where they were going.

The young lad peeked around the corner of the flower mill where he was hiding, there was one particular sail ship, and it was so big it took up most of the quay side.

The British Union Jack was flying high up on her mainmast, there seemed to be a lot of activity around her with sailors loading various items aboard.

William spotted an old sailor, he was sitting on an iron bollard on the quayside smoking a long stemmed clay pipe, he was dressed in a lengthy black frock coat and braided peaked cap, and he seemed to be the only one shouting out the orders.

The boy walked over to him sheepishly saying "hello". "What is it you want boy?" the man abruptly said in a drinkers voice, "I was wondering" said William, "would there be any chance of a job aboard the ship Sir?" The man stood to his full height, pushed his cap back from his forehead, looking very tall he asked the young boy "How old are you?" "Going on sixteen" lied William who was tall for his age. The man looked hard at the boy for a while, then in a dismissive way pointed at the gangplank and said, "Go up there look for the bosun and he'll sort you out".

In his desperation, little did the young lad know, but on that day, by walking up that gangplank he was signing himself into the navy. The ship was a British man of war, having had to replenish her sail's cloth supply from the mills in Douglas, it was then returning to the hell that was the aftermath of the Napoleonic wars.

William would spend two years on board that ship, as a powder monkey and general dog's body who from day one was sent aloft to the crow's nest to act as a look out.

Sailing with new found friends who protected him and low life scum of the earth who threatened to ravage him, eating mostly stale food and drinking sour water that left him in constant danger of picking up the scurvy sickness, the only constant he could rely on was the tot of rum at the end of the day.

In the end Billy Boy as he was then nicknamed for short, felt lucky to be still alive after all the hair raising conflict's on the high seas, constantly counting his blessings to be still in possession of all his limbs, and a sane coherent mind. During a period of shore leave at Southampton docks, with just a handful of sovereigns in his pocket and the cloths on his back, Billy Boy was still fully aware he couldn't return to Ireland he being a wanted man. So he jumped ship with his closest friend, a Glasgow Scott who had been originally press ganged into the navy. They both secretly signed on with a New Bedford whaler that was immediately heading off to the coldest regions of the wild Atlantic

It was a time in his life where Billy Boy developed an angry aversion towards his fellow men, especially whalers, seeing for the first time the callous way those graceful mammals were slaughtered turned his stomach, even though he had become somewhat hardened to death in the navy, it seemed to hurt him more watching those poor graceful giants forced to go through an agonizing death, soulfully keening until they succumbed to the mortal wounds of the harpoons.

One day Billy Boy's best friend, the Scot, through the negligence of a drunken whaler got entangled in the ropes that ran from the ship to the harpoon stuck in the mammal, he was dragged under never to be seen again.

When the ship docked in New Bedford to off load its catch, Billy Boy grabbed his pay and left. He was now in a hurry to leave that God forsaken whaling port. The stench of carcass's was over powering and the memory of his friend's death was heavy on his heart, so he travelled by horse drawn carriage on the long journey to the great metropolis of New York. The Big Apple as New York was loosely called was teeming with people of every colour and nationality, all, it seemed trying to make their fortune.

Billy Boy now had some money in his pocket that gave him a sense of security, so he took a room in a cheap hotel while deciding on what his next plan should be. Having developed a bit of a lip for the rum, from his time in the navy, Billy Boy spent most of the time in the next weeks drinking in one ale house or another. He felt it was where he had the best chance of picking up work.

On one of those evenings when he was walking back from a tavern in China town, deep in a world of his own, he heard screaming coming from one of the narrow side lanes, on investigating the commotion he discovered two drunken tramps holding a young girl forcefully to the ground, in the process of molesting her.

Since he had fled Cork City, and because of all the physical labour he had to endured, Billy Boy had put on muscle he wasn't that scrawny boy anymore, and could stand up for himself with the best of them.

Remembering his mother, punch's flew from fists that were now iron hard, in an instant the tramps lay unconscious in a bloody heap as Billy Boy bent down to give comfort to the crying girl.

*   *   *

The rough wooden table was cluttered with plates of food, Billy Boy sat there already full, he couldn't eat another bite, but still the two people standing alongside of him urged him to eat more, the girl Mai Li sat next to him laughing with joy.

The young girl who Billy Boy had saved from being defiled was Chinese. He had protectively brought her home, and hence he was now sitting in her parent's small restaurant where they couldn't do enough to reward him. Li's eating house was the name over the door. After coming over from Hong Kong, the two parents still only spoke Cantonese, their broken English wasn't great. The young girl done all the translating. The father explained to Billy Boy that if the young girl had been defiled, she would be dishonoured, and would never find a husband and would never carry on the Li name. Billy Boy had saved face for Mr. Li, the family owed him big time.

Mai Li spoke to Billy Boy, she said her father would like to show his appreciation in the traditional way, she said her father was offering the hospitality of his house to Billy Boy for as long as the young man would be in New York, he could have free board and live with the Li family.

*　*　*

Billy Boy was smiling as he whistled an old Irish diddy, he and Mai Li were sitting at the timber table busy preparing food for the restaurant, she laughed when he told her about his mother teaching him all the Irish songs when he was young.

After three weeks staying with the Li's and they treating him like a king, Billy Boy felt guilty, so he brushed their protests aside and helped with their work load, he was loving every minute of it especially the time chatting to Mai, it was the kind of family

62

environment that was doing wonders for his soul.

Six months had passed and Billy Boy was still living with the Li's, but now he had become an integral part of the family, helping Mr. Li in the kitchen, he was now doing some of the cooking and had introduced some simple dish's like porridge and potato skins filled with anything of your choice that were going down a treat with the customers.

Li's eating house was seeing a definite upturn in its business.

Within a matter of two years life had brought so much happiness to Billy Boy he found it hard to believe his luck, from the day he rescued Mai Li from a faith worse than death, she saw him as her knight in shining armour, he was the man she wanted to be with.

Old man Li and his wife were over the moon when Billy Boy asked for Mai's hand in marriage, they loved him like a son, and he in turn treated them like his parents, so it was a match made in heaven.

They were four sitting around the timber table by the light of the lantern, old man Li and his wife, Billy Boy and Mai, the restaurant was closed, this meeting was too important for them to be disturbed.

Even though Billy Boy could speak and understand a lot of the Cantonese language at that stage, for this important meeting Mr. Li insisted that Mai would be there ready to translate if needed.

Mr. Li began, as a form of dowry on the occasion of the upcoming wedding between Billy Boy and Mai, he would hand over a half share of the restaurant to the newlyweds.

Billy Boy and Mai would have full control on the running of the establishment and Billy Boy's own name would be over the door, Mr. Li and his wife would go back to helping in the kitchen preparing the food, happy to stay in the back ground.

*　　*　　*

The group of people standing in Cork's Coal Quay near Saint Peters market were about a hundred, ranging from the very young to the very old, some were dressed in traditional Chinese garments while others wore modern European style's, the one defining factor among them was that nearly all had red hair.

The Buddhist monk stood in the middle of the group, burning holy symbolic money for the repose of the soul of the dead. This was a very solemn occasion, a brass plate was already secured to the wall of the house where Billy Boy had been born, and it was temporarily covered by a short silk curtain.
Many of his descendants were, over from America to honour the occasion. The curious crowds passing by in the market were looking on in amazement.

*　　*　　*

When Billy Boy passed away at the age of 102, all of New York's China town stopped to pay their respects. In the restaurant trade he had been a phenomenal success, everybody knew him, in his life he was the proud father of twelve children, this to the delight of old man Li. When each of those children got married, they were giving the present of their own restaurant, resulting in there being eating houses all over the New England area with Billy Boy's name over the door. Adopting to wearing Chinese style clothing all his life and donning a long red pony tail, Billy Boy became a genius at knowing what people wanted to eat, mixing European dishes with Asian.

In the course of his life he made so much money he almost had a licence to print it, providing food for the ordinary folk at affordable prices.

His weekend specials of all you can eat for a set price, were constantly availed of by many large families.

With burning joss sticks in their hands the gathered group of Chinese kowtowed reverently before joining in the holy chants with the Buddhist monk. Then slowly the brass plaque was unveiled to the delight of the gathered group. The inscription on it was written in both English and Cantonese. It said:

"In honour of our beloved forefather, Billy Boy who was born on this spot 105 years ago.
We will always love and remember you."

Time

The older you get,
the faster time moves.
So rise with the dawn,
or the more time you'll lose.

Randolph Scott in the Cavalry Scout

"What time will we head off?" said Donie to me. "There's no hassle" I told him "We can take the short cut down through Bonties bog and we'll be there in plenty time." "How much have you?" I ask Donie in an over inquisitive tone. "I have four pence from the waste paper money and me mother gave me another two pennies he answered triumphantly." "Where sound so says I we have enough to buy brust on the way home." "Brilliant boy" said Donie punching his fist triumphantly in the air. We'd been anxiously waiting for this movie for a whole week, ever since we saw the trailer out in the Lido cinema.

Next week's coming attraction it announced in large bold letters across the big white screen, the legendary Randolph Scott riding high in the saddle, in a brand new western adventure, the movie everyone is talking about, the academy award nominated, CAVALRY SCOUT. Everyone would try to get out to Blackpool for the Saturday matinee. They'd arrive from all points of the compass, and some would come with only half the entrance fee and take a chance on tapping for the rest outside the door.

That gang would ask anyone for money. Others would come with no money at all, playing the old trick, waiting by the side door, hoping that someone on the inside would open it, then in a flash they'd rush in. The cinema had long wooden bench's for seating, well-worn and shiny from generations of posterior's, we'd usually be jam packed in like a bunch of sardine's and you'd have to be well aware of the odd stab from an errant splinter, a direct result of some scallywag gouging out the wood with his sharp penknife.

Affectionately referred to as the flea pit, the popular saying at the time was that if you went into the Lido a cripple, chances were you'd come out walking. But looking back now, in the overall scheme of things we didn't really care as long as we could live in the make belief world of a child's imagination for a couple of hours.

Setting out for the Lido we were in the best of form, we were going to see our screen hero the great Randolph Scott. Cowboy of cowboy's and western legend.

Going through the rough terrain of Bonties bog we had taken off our shoe' and sock's to cross the fast running stream. We'll play boats for a while I suddenly suggested to Donie "Sure we have plenty time, the movie won't start till three." So we played boats, in the innocent actions of two young kid's, putting bits of wood and twig's into the fast running water to see who's would float the fastest.

Nobody had a watch back then, it was considered a luxury, and being so preoccupied with our fun and game's we'd lost track of time until we came to a unanimous decision that we should to be on our way.

When you were a kid back then and your mother thought you were responsible enough to go to the cinema without adult protection, it gave you the false impression that you were all grown up. When we eventually came in sight of the Lido cinema and saw such a large queue of people we got a terrible fright. "We'll never get in boy" Donie shout's to me. "I told ya we shouldn't have played boats", I answered back, defending myself and trying to shift the blame over to him.

After what seemed like an eternity we got as far as two from the door, when the man wearing the faded captain's uniform roar's in a mechanical voice, House full, next showing Eight O C tonight. What could we do, I ask ya in the name of God what could we do? Donie wise ass that he always was volunteered the perfect answer. "I'll tell ya what we'll do" he said, "If we keep all of our money and don't buy no brust, we'll have enough for the show tonight."

It was a brilliant idea cause in any case the show would be gone after that day. But says I "We can't go home, cause if we do they won't let us out again." Donnie's quick thinking came to the rescue once more, problem solved he said. "We'll go back up to Bonties bog and play more boats and keep watching Shandon to know the time." It was the brainwave of a genius, cause at five past eight that night we were sitting comfortably in the Lido cinema watching our great cowboy hero Randolph Scott shooting at everything and anything that moved, and he strutting around high in the saddle on his Palomino coloured stallion, the epitome of cool.

In our eyes that night he was the greatest cowboy that ever lived, he had it all, from then on a cowboy was what we definitely wanted to be when we grew up. Leaving the Lido that night after watching such a fabulous movie we were still in the land of cowboy fantasy. Outside the front door of the Lido we jumped up on two imaginary Palomino horses conveniently tied up to the local bus stop, maybe they belonged to some of the renegade cowboys Randolph Scott had shot in the movie. We rode like bats out of hell on those wild horses, rode all the way towards our homes, and even though it was the darkest of night's it felt pure magical.

The horses to their credit jumped the fast flowing stream in Bonties bog with the littlest of bother, not even stopping to drink the water, continuing on the onward journey at a steady gallop. Eventually getting home after shooting so many cats and dogs and any other wild animal we encountered, we had to dismount to go in the front doors of our respective houses. Leaving the imaginary horses to run free out on our road. I walked to the front door of my house, it was locked, so I had to knock. The door was jerked open in a flash of light and who's standing there the fire of anger in her eyes, only my mother.

My mother's hand shoots out like the speeding bullet from a high velocity gun and I get such a hot stinging clatter that I don't know if its day or night. "Where were you all night?" she shouts in a raging roar, spittle ejecting from her opened mouth, "You're out since one a clock today and the guards are looking for you and Donie all over Cork City."

"I. I. I. We were out in the Lido Randolph Scott was on" I stammered in an incoherent stutter, "I'll give you the blasted Lido boy", my mother shouts, dragging me in the front door and banging it shut with the force of aggression. "Get straight up to bed" she shouted, "you'll get no dinner in this house tonight, cause it went cold hours ago and I fed it to the chicken". With that I got another side winding clatter that was worse than the first, a stinging clatter that sent me running as fast my skinny legs could carry me, running in such a confused state up the narrow stairs, nearly pissing in my short pants as I ran into the back bedroom, jumping into the bed with all my clothes on and completely covered myself with all the blankets.

After an eternity of fitfully crying my eyes out in the darkness I finally drifted off to the land of nod, a sleep that was full of cowboy dreams and nightmares of clatters. And in the middle of that hazy twilight world I dreamt a magical dream. I dreamt that Me, Donie and our great cowboy hero Randolph Scott were out riding horses and shooting at everything and anything that moved, all over the vast bogs and wild badlands of the Bonties prarier.

Faith

But in the end, I'd have to say,
twas faith brought me around.
It gave me strength, held my hand,
put my feet back on the ground.
I'd never thought, that this could be,
in this old crazy world.
When all my life, since I've been lost,
twas faith helped me be found.

The Fisherman's Lament

The storm was raging now, tossing the little clinker built boat around like a cork. The two men were soaked to the skin from the driving rain. It was pitch dark out here near Roches Point on the edge of the harbour and that's the way they preferred it, not wanting to be spotted by any of those blasted bailiffs. The only fear the two men had now was of getting run down by some large cargo ship.

They were fishing in the deep water channel, the best place to catch the fish, but it was a constant fight to avoid being pushed out to sea, the current was so strong. Periodically the old man looked around, having to take his bearings from the lighthouse beacon on Roches Point.

The two men, father and son came from the nearby town of Cobh, making extra cash by illegally catching fish. The old man was a hardened hand to the game, being doing it all his life, the son Sam had a tendency to be lazy letting the old man do most of the grafting. Sam didn't really want to be out here, he would much more prefer to be in one of the seedy pubs along the waterfront supping Guinness with his mates. But with no work to be found and the dole a pittance Sam had no choice but to be out here, he needed the extra cash, he had a wife and kids to support. Many of his mates had immigrated to England or further afield to the USA but that wasn't an option his wife was in favour of.

The father was blue in the face from berating his son because he turned up drunk, making a nuisance, saying how much he missed his wife and kids, but the old man knew in his heart the young lad was only missing the pub where he spent most of his money.

The old man was at this time of his life living on his own, his wife having passed away twelve years previous, still living in the old family cottage he was for the most part, contented, he could survive well enough on the old aged pension. It covered his tobacco and couple of pints, but from an early age he had the sea water in his blood, and out here on the harbour, was where he still felt most alive.

They would have to spend long hours out on the water, and still it was touch and go if they caught anything that was worthwhile. Any catch they made would be quickly bough up back in the town, the local restaurant or the chipper would grab it, but the price paid was always small, what could ya do when the catch was illegal.

After spending most of the darkened hours out on the harbour where they drank poiten to stay warm, the pink rays of dawn was starting to raise its head over the far off horizon, this was the signal to go, at that stage the storm had hours ago blown itself out. When they headed back towards the town, riding on the crest of the incoming rushing tide, they didn't even have to use the oars. The out board engine was only used as a last resort, its echo carried like an alpine yodeler out here on the water attracting all the wrong ears. Young Sam was now laid back on the stern of the boat, exhaustedly sleeping and noisily snoring.

Pushing his black peaked cap to the back of his head the old man looked to the far off lights of the town, smoking on a full pipe of tobacco, content now with his lot, as the in rushing waters of the wild Atlantic carried the little boat back to the safety of the harbour town.

Owing of the advent of old age and also because he had done this trip thousands of times since he was a young boy, these days the old man had a tendency to nod off on the inward journey.

At the bend of the river where the naval base has been housed for centuries, the large container ship came on at speed, high on the water, her containers were now empty on the return leg to Rotterdam. The Cork pilot who would take the massive ship half a nautical mile beyond the Roches Point lighthouse, saw only the reflection of a black oily sea on front of him, as he steered through the dark. The angry wash from the ships bulbous bow hit the little boat with a savage ferocity, lifting it up and holding it in a vice like grip against the bow. The ship carried on like that, twined with little timber boat until it stopped out at sea to let the pilot off, he was to travel back to Cobh on the launch that pulled alongside. It was only then that the massive ship released the little boat, letting it slip off its bow to sink silently under the salty waves, and taking with it the remains of the two dead fishermen, father and son, down through eerie darkness to the bed of the wild Atlantic ocean.

Seems Like Yesterday

St Patrick's Day is here again,
the green is all around.
The shamrock's selling in the streets,
where people still abound.
The days are moving by so fast,
though it seems like yesterday.
When father took me by the hand,
to walk the old coal quay.

The Father

Johnnies father was a quiet man, that's how he remember him, kept himself to himself most of the time. There was nine of them in family, Johnny was the second youngest, so maybe when he came along, his dad was old.

Looking back now he could recall the mother as being the real boss, she'd probably inherited it from her own mother, a domineering woman, he was led to believe. So most likely from an early stage in the marriage, the father had taken a back seat.

An emotional incident that was forever impregnated in the archives of his mind, was when the mother was away in England. A rushed visit brought on because her three teenaged daughters had started to run wild in the big smoke of Liverpool. It was Johnny, his dad and a younger brother who were left to hold the fort in their corporation house on the north side of Cork City. One day out of the blue the old man said to Johnny, "This is a very lonely house, I don't know why anyone would want to stay in such a lonely house as this."

It was one of the few times the father showed his true feelings, he was missing his wife badly, even missing her being in control.

The father would sometimes take the young lad to the city, he in his dark suit and dark peaked cap and polished shoes, and barely a word would be said between them, they were happy just being in each other's company.

With his hand held in a protective grip, Johnny would be racing along to keep in pace, wearing a short school pants that displayed a pair of white knees and two elf like ears sticking out like the orange indicators of a an old Ford Model T. The lad was forever fascinated by the two metal bridges spanning the river Lee seated right on front of the City Hall. Full of hidden mysteries and harbouring a dangerous life force all of their own.

To an orchestrated sound of grinding steel, part of one would swing open like an enormous Aladdin's gate, the other would crack in half with a thunderous roar and proudly point its giant metal span to the sky. That was the time when shipping vessels could sail unhindered all the way up the River Lee docking at the quayside by the old labour exchange. They could spend hours of contentment there, lazing in silence on the sun parched timber wharf dreaming. Johnny deep in the fairytale world of a little boy's imagination. The fathers friend's used to hang around that area, congregating like a bunch Roman senators, talking with their heads bent low, debating, as a matter of the utmost urgency, important world politics, while at the same time, having no qualms in scrounging a stale woodbine butt or a casual pinch of black snuff.

The toxic aroma of cigarette smoke, would hang in a stagnant white cloud, shrouding those playing don, or those in a deep forlorn trance. All the men seemed to be wearing the same dark suits and peaked caps back then, flagrantly donned as if it were some kind of obligatory uniform.

But in retrospect maybe they were really just killing time. When the father's dole day came round he'd usually give the young lad a big treat, a giant ice cream from the polo ice cream shop at the end of the South Mall. This cold slab, sandwiched between two thin crispy wafers was the epitome of pleasure.

More ice than cream, it was so big it could hardly be held between the young lad's fingers.

Running down the back of the hand, it ending up dripping from the tip of his elbow like a crystal stalactite. As it melted there would be a ferocious race against time, licking at an ever increasing speed, in a quest to devour it. The cold shivers of pain shooting frozen darts through his spinal cord was only a minor discomfort, as the last lumps of ice cream were consumed, leaving sticky fingers, white lips a bulging belly, and all it had cost was the couple of large brown pennies.

Maybe he was around seven years old, it was the time his father had picked up three weeks part time work down the docks, swaging large canvas bags of grain in the flour mill. The mother took him and the younger brother down to the father's place of work, he was paid on a midday Friday, so he gave her some money at the mill's main gate, and he looked like a church yard ghost, standing there covered from head to foot in white flour. Johnny remembered him as a frail old man back then, skeletal thin and bent over, he shouldn't have being lifting heavy bags of grain at that stage of his life, but then again maybe the extra money was badly needed.

He handed over five green one pound note's to the mother and without saying a word, turned around and walked back into the dark cavern of the mill.

Johnny didn't know or care about what problems two adults had in trying to feed and clothe a large family back then, all he was concerned about that day, in his own self-centered way, was the milk and cakes he was about to eat in the small cafe in Parnell Place.

But as the old saying goes:
"time wait's for no man"

The father died when Johnny was about to enter the teenage years, at that stage he was busy in the little hip world of self-importance. Looking back now Johnny thought, there was in any case a big generation gap after developing, in that strange relationship between an aged father and his young son, and all those years where words were left unsaid.
Or had it always been there. Johnny wishes now they could have talked more to each other, he thinks deep down they had a lot to say. But all of his life the father was just a quiet man, kept himself to himself.
Johnny would have loved to know more about the father's early life and all the local history that went with it, it would have been great if he had written it all down.
The old man is a long time gone now, a lot of water has flowed under that rickety bridge, and sitting there in the autumn of his life kept Johnny constantly reminiscing and left with the one regretful thought.....he never really knew his father.

Health is Wealth

Clouds of crimson clouds of white,
sun that makes the heavens bright,
a perfect day makes all things right,
for all with eyes to see it.
A dove is calling from a roof,
to me it seems it's just more proof,
man has wealth when health is good,
for those who've come to known it.

Red Wine

Baker's lane ran down from the top of Cathedral road, all the way to Blarney Street, a rustic cobbled stoned incline, with a slow flowing stream on the left side and a high limestone wall, covered with deep rooted ivy on the right.

Enclosing the grounds of the monastery, this eight foot high barrier was pock marked with weather beaten holes, where over the span time, generations of small birds learned to build their nests.

The collage inside this wall on the north side of Cork city, was a prominent seat of religious learning for novice monks, sent there to study and prepare for the harsh life of monastic celibacy.

With a relaxed patience, the four teenagers, deep in conversation, stood with their backs leaning against the old wall, waiting under the swinging shade of a dimed street lamp, at the T-junction of the hill.

A scraping movement alerted their attention to a lanky youth, jumping from the top of the wall, and landing gracefully beside them, a roguish smile on his young face, silently he gave a brief nod while extracting a long slim bottle from inside his donkey jacket, holding it up triumphantly in an act of bravado he playfully laughed, saying, " Red wine fresh from the altar."

Quickly removing its cork, the five lads took long generous slugs till the contents was greedily emptied. The bottle was then carelessly broken against the base of the wall.

"Where we going?" enquired the late arrival with a familiar shrug his bony shoulders.

Pushing back the scruffy peaked cap, perched at a devil may care angle on his blond mop, he took half a cigarette from behind his left ear, then scratching a match against the lime stone wall, he commenced to light up, with the practiced skill of an expert.

Kerry Joe was a novice monk. He had been christened Kerry Joe by his friends because he was a native of Tralee, had been living in the monastery for the past six months, but in reality he was the wildest of birds who vehemently swore every day, he'd never be caged.

His brother and sister were already at that stage priest and nun, born into a poor family and pushed into the holy orders against their wills, destined to serve in some God forsaken backwater on the other side of the globe, all because at the time it was the fashion, done by misguided parents to gain brownie points for an easy ride into heaven, and to craw thump at mass on a Sunday.

Kerry Joe was automatically expected to follow the same road, but he was having none of it, the rebel in him constantly wouldn't conform, he was forever getting himself into trouble because he wouldn't knuckle down and study.

It was a regular occurrence for him to sneak out at night and scale the perimeter wall, where he'd meet with his new found buddies from the corporation estate.

Chip, Wally, Billa and Wacker, four tear ways who weren't afraid of anything the world could throw at them.

They'd be out stealing the tinkers horses from the nearby halting site, going on exhilarating bare backed rides across open green fields and narrow furze lined lanes, getting into adult card schools that were held in the sloping quarry off Barret's buildings, where if you had a good win, you were well fixed to buy a couple of large bottles of scrumpy cider and woodbine cigarette's.

Of late, in a show of flagrant daring, Kerry Joe was taking the gang back over the monastery wall, in the darkness of night he would lead them to the prized orchard, the fenced enclosure where hung the award winning eating apple's, painstakingly nurtured to prize winning fruition by the old gardener monks.

The culprits would only bite into the best juicy ones, leaving a trodden trail of half eaten cores on the ground, in the blatant show of youthful defiance. Hanging around with the local girls from Blarney Street was stirring emotions in the young Kerry man that was a whole new adventure, desperately wanting to progress beyond the kiss and the cuddle, made it obviously clear to him, he could never go through life in a state of celibacy. Joe's new found thirst for living was making him the wildest of the gang, the bird set free now encompassed life outside the lime stoned wall with both hands.

On Saturday nights, dressed in one of Billa's light blue teddy boy suits with the velvet collar, and his hair oiled back in a ducks ass in the fashion of the day, he and the rest of his buddies would head off to the city, where he'd dance the night away, canoodling with all the pretty girls, under the soft romantic lights of the Gresham Rooms.

Smelling of alcohol and stale nicotine, regularly keeling over half asleep at the obligatory Sunday morning six o clock mass, usually brought strange looks of derision from Joe's fellow novices in the monastery's little church. Joe's mother was summoned up to Cork City all the way from her little thatched cottage outside Tralee, the monastery's brother superior informed her that her son didn't seem to have his whole heart set on becoming a servant of the lord, wasn't applying himself hard enough to his clerical studies.

In a lambasting fit of rage, spitting fire and brimstone, the mother tore into Joe, ordered him to quickly change his attitude, settle down and learn, and not to be bringing total disgrace on her good family name, she was worried about what the neighbours back in Kerry might say.

"What about me Ma?" said Joe, "It's my life where talking about here, shouldn't I have the right to choose what to do with it." His mother took the first bus back to Kerry red eyed from crying, angry that her son should be so insensitive and disrespectful to her wishes for him to go into the holy order of Christ, like his brother and sister. Oh she thought, the mortification and embarrassment of it all, facing the stares and snide remarks from the neighbours, after all the boasts she made about having three children in the clergy, she wouldn't be able to live with the shame of it.

But it was already too late for Joe, he had truly booted celibacy out the door, with his coming over the wall and partying till the early hours with the help of his buddies from the north side. Joe's fortune took a drastic turn, things seemed to happen in a flash.

Nan one of the girls who hung out with the Blarney street crowd and who seemed to have taken a fancy to Joe became pregnant. After her father had angrily threatened he'd have her locked up in Bessborough if she didn't tell who put her with child, tearfully she blabbed the whole story.

Pointing the finger at Joe she said they were madly in love, that for months they had been involved in a wild passionate affair, unbeknownst to even their closest friends.

After that it was the fastest shotgun wedding in the history of the north side.

Joe awkwardly standing there next to Nan wearing Billas blue Teddy boy suit, in the claustrophobic sacristy of the local church, this been of a time when a man felt compelled to do the honourable thing and stand by the woman. Billa nervously fingering the barn brack ring in his waistcoat pocket, and one of Nan's girlfriends from Blarney Street, were the only witnesses in the little group of four.

After the brother superior was informed of Joe's clandestine escapades, with stealth precision the young Kerry man was instantly expelled, walking out the gate, carrying his meagre possessions in a small brown case.

When Kerry Joes mother heard the shameful news she reverted into a state of piousness and complete denial, to the point where she cut off all forms of human contact, completely abandoning and disowning her son in a silent rage.

The newlyweds were given shelter by Billa's mother, her heart went out to them in their hour of need, she fed them and gave them the comfort of her house, treating them like one of her own, and the two young people never showed their faces outside the door for the best part of a week.

Money for their fares on the Innisfallen was raised by the girl's father, Joe had the promise of a job at the Ford's motor plant in Dagenham England.

Waving goodbye to their friends on the Cork dockside brought on tears of open emotion, as in the driving rain the newlyweds clung to each other on the deck of the wind swept ship, against their wishes, they were been shipped off to England.

Out of sigh out of mind, where the shame would be far enough away from the vicious gossipmongers, and the long pointing finger of the local parish priest.

Vulnerable and bound for a foreign land, they were now left to fend for themselves.

* * *

The five grey old men sat at the round table in the Temple Acre Tavern, a well know watering hole on Corks north side. The table was littered with empty pint glasses and cartons of half eaten fish and chips.

Well into their pension age now it was really a miracle they all had survived to be sitting here, wild men in their days, always bucking the trend, and in many ways still doing it in old age.

Chip and Wally had been army men all their lives, seen action from the Congo to Beirut and wore the scars to prove it, but being two true Norries all their lives, they always returned to live on the north side.

Billa lived in England for many years before he eventually returned to set down roots in his wife's home city of Limerick. He never really came back to Cork to live again, a grandfather now, living out his days walking his dogs in the city of the treaty stone. Wacker was a wino, since a teenager he had taken to the drink, wandering the major cities of Ireland and England without care or purpose in a drunken stupor.

And Kerry Joe wheelchair bound for the last three years who was plagued by creeping arthritis, but still because of his strong Kerry heritage, fiercely independent. He had only been too happy to fly all the way over from his home in Sidney Australia, to once again sit and reminisce in the company of his dear old friends.

With the easy stride of an athlete, the striking young blond girl walked back from the bar counter looking as graceful as a model, which she was. Balancing the tray of drinks on the tips of her fingers she approached the five old men, stood before them and put the drinks on their table.

Looking over at Joe sitting in his mobile chair with a warm rug over his legs, the young girl said in a broad Australian accent and a smile of deep affection on her face, yours is a pint of Guinness grand dad, and kissing him on the top of the head, she carefully placed the white headed drink on the table before him.

It had been young Nan's persistent endeavor that made this reunion possible, named after her late grandmother, the twenty year old was a whizz kid at the internet, and over the last twelve months she religiously tracked down all the old friends to make this Irish gathering possible.

Wacker was the biggest problem, of no fixed abode, a hardened drifter who even as an old man, still slept rough in any convenient doorway, when he couldn't find bed space in a city hostel.

Nan had made contact with an old internet friend in the Galway Gardaí, and in answer to her enquiries, he texted her to say Wacker was staying in the local hostel. She quickly emailed a message to have Wacker told to try and find his way back to Cork for the reunion, crossed her fingers in an act of faith, hoping the old man would be able to make the journey.

The grandniece had also volunteered, she wanted to be the one to travel with her grandfather when he flew over to Ireland.

Moving slowly through the evenings fading light, the minibus stopped outside Billas old corporation house. Looking its age now, it seemed much smaller than Joe remembered.

A new family lived there now, Billas clan had been for a long time, scattered to the four winds of time. Holding back the tears Joe looked up at the small bedroom window, remembering that he and his late wife Nan spent their honeymoon there, was it really all those years ago that Billas mother went out of her way to make them feel loved and wanted. In his clearness of mind it seemed like only yesterday.

Reading his far off thoughts, his young niece bent down and gave him the warm comfort of a protective lingering hug.

Closing his eyes now Kerry Joe could still remember the terrible fear in his young wife's eyes as they walked down the gangway at Fishguard docks, and they both full of apprehension entering this strange land. Joe knew he had nothing but good to say about the English, they were the best of friends to him, they were always willing to make that effort and help him and his pregnant wife make a home, forever showing true Christian compassion.

After three homesick years Joe became a qualified spray painter, making good money in the Dagenham plant. Living in a three roomed flat with his wife and two year old daughter in deep harmonious love, he was well liked by his friends because of his infectious nature.

Then out of the blue another life changing opportunity beckoned, the family decided to take the offer of the emigration package, and were transferred to the Ford Motor Company in sunny Australia. Kerry Joe lived a contented life in Aus., truly becoming an integral part of that country, rearing a large family who gave him many grandchildren, eventually opening his own spray painting shop which he proudly named Kerry Joe's.

In an ironic twist of fate, Joe was practically a lay priest now. Over the years he'd been more and more drawn into the faith, constantly feeling the need to help in his local church, counselling, making life that little bit easier for the droves of new Irish emigrants to settle in Sidney, and was constantly there to help give out the holy communion at Sunday mass, in spite of been wheelchair bound.

Gathered under the yellow glow of the ancient street lamp, the five old aged pensioners gazed at the limestone wall, it had once formed the boundary to the monastery, and it was still standing after all those years, even though parts of it had crumbled down. The monastery was now long gone, converted to modern apartments, houses dominated the old grounds as far as the eye could see, not a trace of an orchard or an apple tree in sight.

The five old friends stood there silently, staring, as if paying their final act reverence. A homage to Jerusalem's wailing wall. A rustling sound cut through the eerie stillness

Kerry Joe took five plastic cups from the large paper bag, hanging from the side of his wheelchair, handed four of them to his old mates and keeping one for himself.

Pulling a long slim bottle out of the bag. He held it up for the others to see in the dusk of the streetlamp.

And with the broadest of smiles on his craggy old face, the Kerry man said.

"Red wine, fresh from the alter"

Music's in my veins

I've travelled many lonely roads,
in search of lady fame.
Played in places so obscure,
trying hard to make a name.
Doing country, Irish, 60s rock,
I loved to entertain.
Cause it's forever in my blood,
yes, musics in my veins.

Annie

Annie never knew her mother, after she was born down in Bessborough the home where young girls went to have their babies out of wedlock. Annie was immediately handed over to an obese nun who was the in-house wet nurse and put straight into the adoption ward.

Donning a full head of fiery red curls when she was born, the infant had the lungs of an opera singer when in need of milk.

An ugly baby because she had the affliction of a hair lip, plus the head of red unkempt hair, made her, in the reverend mother's opinion a definite turn off to prospective parents. This resulted in little Annie being shunted to the far corner of the adoption ward, discreetly camouflaged behind the green plastic screen.

After nine long months of been cared for by the nuns of Bessborough who christened her "nobody's child", Annie was eventually handed over to the home for unwanted babies, up in the Good Shepard's Convent at the top of Sundays Well. She was then destined to spend the next seventeen years of her life in the convent, toiling for long hours from a very young age in the workhouse laundry. Annie shared her daily grind with dozens of other orphaned children, like herself, working under the strict order of those religious nuns. Forever dressed in simple child's clothing, a long grey unfeminine smock and clogs for footwear, reciting prayers every other hour while donning a pressed down bonnet, her wiry red hair now cropped to the bone, the deformity of a hair lip forcing her to talk with a lisp even as a teenager, never ever really knowing what the outside world was like from the day she was born.

By the time she reached the age of seventeen, Annie was completely institutionalized.

* * *

When the Greenmount Correctional School for Boys on the south side of Cork City suddenly closed its doors for the final time, some of its occupants were temporarily housed in the Good Shepard's Convent resulting in a serious case of overcrowding. To solve this problem the nuns took drastic action. They quickly found live in jobs around Cork City and beyond for some of the older orphaned girls, literally pushing them out the door to the outside world, left to fend for themselves in an alien environment for the first time in their young innocent lives.

Annie was totally confused now, lost and afraid, ending up toiling as a skivvy in a sweaty hotel kitchen, treated like a simpleton, to be at everyone's beck and call, the butt of incessant insults. Her hair lip which she tried to disguise by constantly putting her hand over her mouth and a now red unkempt afro mop, making the girl easy prey because of her quite vulnerable nature

After eating the frugal meal provided by the hotels Chinese chef, she would silently climb the rickety staircase to the tiny attic room at twelve midnight, there to fall on jaded knees and pray to an invisible God for forgiveness for being such a constant sinner during the day, before finally collapsing onto the single mattress to sleep the troubled sleep of the exhausted.

The poor girl was the hotels comical misfit, didn't know how to dress properly or socialize in other people's company and she going round muttering silent prayers under a hand covered breath. On Sundays when she had the luxury of a day off, Annie rose early to attend six o clock mass at St Mary's on the quay, with eyes shut tight, meditating on bony knees in the loneliness of an overcrowded pew.

Then when service was finally over, trekking off on the long slog up to the Good shepherds Convent to visit her old friends and once again feel at home.

But the nuns in their indifference soon put a stop to those unwelcome visits.

First when the poor girl started to stay longer in the familiar environment and finally after she asked to be allowed to come back into the convent because she couldn't live in the outside world anymore.

The giant mahogany doors of the Good Shepard's Convent were then permanently closed in Annie's face, making her feel like the loneliest person in the world. Like a lost lamb Annie now found her time off on a Sunday hard to fill, she took total refuge in her religion, going to one mass after another, spending long hours on her aching knees doing self-inflicted penance for being such a bad person.

The young woman was trying hard to stay away from the ominous attraction of the quayside wall, where her mind was filled with morbid thoughts as she stared hypnotically into the deep rushing waters of the river Lee.

It was a chance glance at the notice board hanging on the back wall of ST MARY's church that held her attention. She had been aimlessly walking around doing the stations, praying with a rosary beads clenched in her white knuckled hands when she spotted it. A special meeting that was to be held in the sacristy of the church on the following Sunday afternoon at four o clock, stating that any young women who were interested in becoming nuns were welcome to come along.

* * *

Annie walked around the walled in garden in a slow silent motion, head covered and dressed in the dark blue smock of a novice, reading from a leather clad bible in deep concentration, hardly taken in the palatial confines of the Rosscarbury convent for trainee nuns. Six months now since she took the vows that married her to the Christen God. They had immediately sent her down to West Cork to work in silence and solitude, expecting her to perform any kind of labouring task she was ordered to. The nuns kept to a strict code of silence in accordance with their vows, lasting for twenty two hours of the day, except when speaking to God while they prayed, it had an initial calming effect on Annie. But as time went by deep down she still felt a nagging loneliness, something was still missing in her life.

Unbeknownst to the young woman, from the first day she stepped foot inside the West Cork convent she was been constantly assessed.

The reverend mother had an experienced eye and she could see the young novice didn't really fit into a silenced order, but she'd be given more time to adjust to the trials and strains, because being married to God wasn't always an easy life.

An open convent in Cork City who cared for deprived children needed a young nun to act as an overseer, she would have to be strong willed and not afraid of the constant grind of hard work.

The reverend mother suggested the position to Annie in a roundabout way of testing her commitment to the West Cork convent.

The young novice was given a week to think it over, told to pray hard to the man above for guidance, but she didn't need the week, and was back after only a day to tell the reverend mother she definitely wanted to leave.

In the hot humid ironing room where the pristine washed linen came to be pressed, twelve young girls in long grey smocks worked with the boiling steam irons, their heads in bonnets and bent in full concentration, they silently smoothing the wrinkles out of the various items that had been washed and dried. A young nun at the top of the long table worked the large presser, her sleeves turned up short and a constant sheen of perspiration covering her pale face and upper arms. It was oppressively hot in the large Victorian room as sister Annie stood through the long hours, working in the steam filled laundry. Watching like a mother hen over the orphaned girls, she uttered a short prayer, now at peace with herself.

Annie was happy to be back again working in the confines of the only home she ever knew-The Good Shepard's Convent.

Mother Nature's Plot

The fox the rabbit and the crow,
the spiny crawling hedgehog
The cow the bull the running horse,
a dove that coos in hawthorn.
The goat the fish the gentle lamb,
or fungis equine trot.
Their all a part of Gods own plan, and mother nature's plot.

The Day Trip

Someone said how's about we go for a day trip, men only, that's how it started. Working down in Henry Fords could be like a prison at times, you couldn't get outside the perimeter fence without the aid of a signed pass, so any chance of breaking the monotony, and you'd grab it with both hands.

For a start, money had to be collected each week from those who were interested in going, it was a way of sorting out the wasters from the committed. When the day finally came we were all in a great mood, our destination was West Cork.

Waiting on the bus for the late comers who finally arrived well drunk after being in some early morning pub, this was a good start. When the bus eventually starts to move off, one of those who are full up with drink suggests we should have one for the road in the Port Bar, with a mob of twenty you knew it would be a lot more than one

Two hours later after a sing song and more people getting drunk, the bus driver says, I think we should be off now lads. So we head off for West Cork, big sing song along the way and many more stops for drinks and leaks.

After arriving at the hotel in Owenahincha for dinner, getting off the bus some head straight for the bar, others can't wait to get on the beach to start a soccer match. There are still a couple of bodies asleep, stretched out on the long seats of the back of the bus, dead to the world. Dinner is now being served, a big round up to get everyone into the dining room, some don't even want a dinner this early in the day. "I have a noble call" someone shouts, some day already.

After an eternity where back on the bus, if we don't move now we'll never get there, this is one of the gang who was playing soccer on the beach, he's covered in sweat and his suit is in a terrible state. We sleep all the way to Cape Clare our next port of call. Waking up we groggily fall out of the bus and onto the ferry boat. The Captain shouts at some of the hard men in the group, who are dangerously bent over the side of the boat getting sick, lads don't fall in there. Landing on the other side we stagger ashore and fall on our knees, suffering from severe bouts of sea sickness after the turbulent movement of the water. Someone says, "this great how they can understand us around here", big laugh, "Were you ever outside Cork City before boy?" Someone else shouts, more laughing. The lads who didn't want dinner back in the hotel are now suddenly starving. Their frantically looking around the island for some place that serves food even a bag of potato crisps. Another soccer match has started, the lads running around like headless chicken, some of them half naked, suits and other items of clothing thrown everywhere on the rocks, it's a boiling hot day and with too much alcohol consumed its coming out in rivers of sweat, the day trippers are knackered.

One by one they lay down on the wet beach, sleeping where they fall, and people passing by are careful to give them a wide berth. A loud shout suddenly brings them out of their stupor, "The last ferry is leaving, if we don't go now were stuck here", panic, panic, panic, there's a mad rush to retrieve the suits and other items of clothing.

Back on the boat no one's talking much, dog tired and they really don't know what day they have.

On the bus back to Cork City no one's singing anymore because every one's asleep. There's an orchestration of snores as we sleep the sleep of the exhausted on the return journey, dreaming, cruising along in the darkness of night, till we eventually get back to the city by the Lee.

The end of a perfect day.

The Three Masted Barque

The white sails kiss the summer breeze,
her bow runs straight and true.
The rigging sings of pearly queens,
and tales of Tim Buc Tu.
Her helms man holds a northern course,
as she plough's the ocean's race.
While seamen dream of Fiddlers Green,
and maiden's sweet embrace.

A Mother's Prayer

Red had his face pressed hard against the rough bars of the jail's window, watching a makeshift scaffold been hurriedly put together by a group of union soldiers. Red felt the shivers of fear, touching the very marrow of his bones.

How did he ever let his life come down to this? He cursed himself for been so stupid.

His two cell mates, hardened Johnny rebs, the crazy bastards were sleeping like babies in their bunks behind him, noisily snoring and emitting the stagnant smell of human sweat that was oppressively over powering. Red closed his sleepless eyes to the sound of nail's been driven into the wooden scaffold, he forced his mind to escape the growing claustrophobia and travel back.

He was a seven year old watching his mother kissing the little straw cross that hung to the side of the front door of their tiny thatched cottage that sat in one of the narrow lanes off Fair hill, in the north side of Cork city, back in the old country. They were after getting evicted, his father having lost his part time job in the Butter Market, they couldn't pay the rent anymore. Red's mother was crying her eyes out, this was the old family house, the only home she'd ever known, and she knew she'd never see it again.

There was just the father the mother and their only child Red, the parents had made the heart breaking decision to immigrate to Wales to try and find work in the mines.

They felt devastated, Ireland having become a barren and destitute land over the years, Cork city was one of the worst. The place was full of starving families driven in from the country side living and begging on the streets. Those who could scrape a few coins together after selling the last of their meagre possessions, headed for the quayside, the high masts of the sailing ships with their open decks, crowded the harbour, émigré's herded on board like cattle, people in a desperate panic to get on board those scurvy riddled ships.

Half afraid to look back, the family slowly made their way down the steep incline of Fair hill, carrying only the clothes they were wearing. It was young Red now in total confusion, who kept looking back up the hill, his mother harshly dragging him by the hand, the lane and the cottage were fast fading out of sight, the young lad crying out that he didn't want to leave his friends. He wanted to run back home.

They stayed with an uncle in a small mining town in Wales, deep in the valleys. Reds father picked up a job alien to his nature. He was paid by what coal he dug out of the ground, slaving away in the claustrophobic atmosphere of the semi darkness to provide food for his family. Red earned extra pennies sorting big lumps from small lumps on the coal tip, working alongside the withered old stagers who's lungs were already rock hard, clogged with the black dust. It was an agonizing labour just for them to take a breath.

After six months of working all the hours they could get and coal dust that seemed to be ingrained into everything, their world was suddenly shattered. Reds mother, after having to constantly cope with debilitating bouts of manic depression contracted tuberculosis. The raking cough eventually sent her to an early grave. She was buried there in the black shale ground by the side of the giant mountain under the shade of a timber cross. Red was barely eight years old then. It was just him and the father left now, the father having turned to the bottle to dampen the fear of going underground, creating a cold unfriendly relationship where they rarely spoke.

After a time the Welsh Mining Company put up notices looking for volunteer miners to work in their mine in Pennsylvania out in America. With the promise of a better standard of living and better money, the old man in his drunkenness made the decision for both of them to go. He wanted a fresh start, some place to forget the bad memories.

They weren't to know then but it would turn out to be a worse hell hole than the one they had left, where the management owned you body and soul. Where it got to the stage you owed the company so much for the use of tools you broke, the clothes on your back, food and where you laid your head. It was like a prison sentence that you could never get out of, and on top of that when you died the debts were passed on to your next of kin.

After four years of that back breaking hell, Red was then twelve going on thirteen working a grown man's shift with the other hardened miners in the bowels of the earth, then a seismic shift in the weakened landscape caused a massive cave in at the coal face, it claimed the life of his alcoholic father.

Surviving the hell hole disaster Red felt there had to be a better life somewhere out there for him, he made a break from the mine in the dark of the night. He had enough of this slave labour, The Company immediately put a price on his head. He was their property. He owed them the money from his father's accumulated debts. Red was now classed as a wanted criminal.

So Red found himself doing any kind of job he could find while keeping his head low because of the company posting wanted notices. It wasn't long before he got into criminal activities, surviving by falling in with gangs of wild nomadic cowboys, living by their own rules, robbing banks, holding up trains and any other low handed con they could find.

Still only a teenaged kid he became fast with a gun like the famous Billy the kid. Mixing with all the wrong people. He was already hardened to life from working down the mines, having to grow up fast. When the American civil war broke out. Because of the rebel in him he wore the grey uniform of the confederacy, where he became a bigger criminal than he had been before, legalized with a free hand and a licence to kill.

War was a good period for Red. Made him feel important, alive, He always had plenty of dollars in his pockets and women for the taking, any bank, north or south was fair game. He was now a mercenary soldier serving with the infamous Quantralls Raiders spreading a reign of terror pillage and raping.

After years of savage fighting the union blue coats won the war, abolished slavery and were hell bent on revenge against the Quantralls gang of killers. They chased and harassed Red and his cronies from state to state. Hanging whoever they caught along the way for crimes of genocide against the America people. Red and two other rebels curly Jack and Vance were hounded day and night, living like animals. They were eventually captured in the state of Kansas after a botched bank job, a saloon prostitute sold them out for the green Yankee dollar and now they were held in this stone fortress, after been sentenced in a blue belly courthouse and facing the hang man's noose.

He could hear his mother's voice talking to him now, chastising him like when he was a child, well Redmond you've come a long way from the old cottage back in Fair hill, he could hear her saying, and every step of it has the devils foot print. He wished once more he could go back to the times he played innocent games with the other children, just a snotty nosed kid with a hole in the arse of his pants never caring about tomorrow. The times his father would take him down to Cork City and treat him to a piece of coloured candy stick, and the big wooden ships on the docks of the river Lee, ships with their giant white masts and the colourful sailors everywhere to be seen. If only he could start all over again. If only. But he was stuck here in this God forsaken jail and all the wishing in the world wouldn't get him out, for all the sorrow, damage and deadly pain he caused to his innocent fellow man, it was now pay back time. The judges words were still ringing loud and clear in his ears, hang them murdering Johnny Reb's by the neck till they stop kicking and then shoot the cowardly bastards in the head.

Tomorrow was the day, and still the other two were sleeping like babies in the timber cots behind him. Had they no fear of death? Or would it be a welcome relief for them.

Red pressed his face harder against the rusting bars of the window, scraping the skin of his forehead, hoping to draw blood and find comfort in the pain, the sound of hammering from the scaffold, was again penetrating like a knife through his brain. He pulled the string he had around his neck from inside his faded shirt, it had a holy medal on it, a gift from his mother when he was a small boy.

He kissed it with tearful eyes and tried to remember the words of the prayer she had taught him back in the old country, so long ago in that little thatched cottage in the narrow lane that ran off of Fair hill. On the north side of Cork city.

The End

Made in the USA
Monee, IL
07 July 2026

56686372R00069